SUNNY VALLEY

A novel by Vince Donovan

SUNNY VALLEY

This is a work of fiction. Names, characters, places and incidents either are the product of the author's imagination or are used fictitiously, and any resemblance to actual persons, living or dead, business establishments, events or locales is entirely coincidental.

Poetry adapted from:
The Complete Poems of Emily Jane Bronte, edited by C.W. Hatfield
Shakespeare's Sonnets, Folger Shakespeare Library Edition, edited by Barbara Mowat and Paul Werstine.

ISBN 978-0-578-02074-7

For Catherine

"She pictures me a hero of romance, expecting unlimited indulgences from my chivalrous devotion…"

Heathcliff

CHAPTER 1

Darla opened her eyes but saw nothing. She touched a hand to her face and then patted over the lumpy comforter, feeling for her husband. The room was black.

"Jason?"

He didn't stir. Darla pressed her lips together, trying to calm her racing heart. She was afraid of the dark. It was stupid, she knew, but it was true.

The noise came again, a sound growing in the darkness of the room, filling her skull. Darla first heard it only moments ago—it had woken her up. It sounded like someone moaning, but there was also an unearthly high squeal that made her skin prickle.

"*Jason.*" Darla pushed at his body, but there was no response. He'd had more than a few shots of Jagermeister down in Pine Butte and Darla had to practically carry him up the Lodge stairs to their room.

Darla sat up and felt for the bedside table. It was *so* dark. She had no idea where the lamps were in the room or the wall switches. She *hated* this about herself. As a girl she'd lain in bed nearly every night staring into the blackness, too afraid to sleep. She got over it eventually, but once in a while something triggered it all again.

"*Jason.*" The sound was growing again. Darla was sure there was something more than just the darkness to be afraid of. She balled up a fist and hit Jason on his hairy shoulder. Again, nothing. What was *wrong* with him? It was crazy, she knew, but the sound seemed to surround their bed. It was rhythmic, almost a chant, growing louder and faster. Darla imagined tall men in black robes incanting horrible devil worship stuff. They would cut out Jason's heart (not that he would even notice after all that

Jagermeister) and then they would ...

Something nipped the comforter near her feet, a momentary but undeniable touch. Darla screamed and threw herself onto Jason's body, calling his name and striking with both fists.

Jason sat up and with one hand swept Darla onto the floor. With the other hand he found the bedside lamp and switched it on.

"Darla?"

Darla lay naked on the old wooden floor, sobbing.

"What's going on Squeaker?" Jason said. "What are you doing?"

Darla folded herself into a ball, her slender arms and legs tucked into each other. Jason climbed out of bed and lifted her to her feet.

"What's the matter?"

"Duh, duh, duh." Darla's chin wobbled up and down.

"It's okay, Squeaker," Jason said. "Get hold of yourself. I'm here. What's wrong? Dreaming about the boogeyman again? I'll protect you."

"Uh, uh, I'm *sorry*. I'm so *stupid*."

"It's okay, Squeaks. You know it's okay."

Darla pressed her lips together hard. She couldn't believe she had let herself get so scared. She hadn't felt like this for years and years.

"*Listen*," Darla said.

"Listen to what?"

She put a hand to his mouth. "Buh, be quiet. I know I'm just being studid, but just be quiet and listen."

They stood together in the middle of the room, Darla wrapped tightly around Jason. He felt her swallowing her sobs, trying to get control of herself, trying to be quiet so that they could hear whatever it was they were supposed to hear. Darla had nightmares sometimes, but never this bad.

Jason looked up and examined a deer antler chandelier that hung overhead. He hadn't seen one of those since his parents first took him skiing in Vermont when he was a kid. Jason had thought it was retro and cool when they checked into the Lodge earlier, but now, standing close to it, he could see it was caked with dust. Tiny cobwebs ran between the antler points. This place was going to need some serious fixing up after Darla's dad bought it, he thought. *Serious* fixing up.

The far wall of the lodge room was made of real logs, stained dark by time. An old photograph hung there. Jason had taken a good look at it before they went to bed. The picture showed a weathered cowboy holding a shotgun and standing knee deep in snow. It was not the most inspiring sight at the moment.

"Darla..."

"*Shhhhh.*" Her face was buried in his neck. The damp of tears spread over his bare shoulder. Then Darla's grip on Jason tightened. There *was* some sort of sound. Jason closed his eyes and listened. Someone moaning. It really did sound close, right in the room practically. And now a screech, or scream. Some super high frequency noise filling the room. It *was* weird.

"What is it, Jason? What is it? Oh, I'm such a *baby.*"

Jason worked his jaw. That little scream. It was weird, but also familiar.

The realization was abrupt. Jason threw up his hands and Darla almost fell to the floor again. He let out a whoop and a laugh. He threw Darla onto the bed, and then sat on the edge, laughing.

"*Jason.*"

For a moment he could only croak. He wiped his eyes, caught his breath and pulled Darla close.

"What is it? Stop *laughing.*"

"I'm sorry Squeaker. It's killing me is all. I know that sound. Boy do I know that sound. It's Ellie."

"Your sister?"

"I guess her room's right under ours." Jason stomped on the pine floor with both feet, beating it like a drum. "HEY," he yelled. "Take it easy down there. Some of us are trying to sleep."

The noise stopped abruptly.

"Is it *really* Ellie? That's all? Just Ellie?"

"Yeah. She's a real moaner. She had her eye on some ski instructor at the bar down in Pine Butte. I guess she rode up with him. Christ, when I was home last summer I had to listen to Ellie and her boyfriend all weekend long whenever Dad and Carol went to Boca. I finally started sleeping in the garage."

Darla sniffed and then slapped her own thigh in frustration. "I can't believe it," she said.

"C'mon Squeaks," Jason said. "We havin' fun now?" He put a finger under her chin and kissed her, but her lips were hesitant, unconvinced. "I guess so," she said. "I'm sorry I woke you up. I can't believe I'm such a crybaby. It was so *dark* in here, though. I mean, I know it sounds stupid but it seemed darker than dark."

"That's just because we're staying somewhere unfamiliar."

"I guess. And then that weird sound filled the room. You were out cold, like you were dead."

Jason chuckled. "I was pretty well medicated."

"I'll say. And then something *touched* me! I totally felt it. I swear something, like, grabbed my foot. Right out of the dark."

Jason looked around. "This lodge is a piece of shit. Someone should just toss a match in the place. Why does your dad want to buy into it?"

"I dunno." Darla sighed and wiped her eyes. "A project for Kyle, I guess."

"As if. If your dad gives this resort to your jackass brother it really will burn to the ground. Your dad doesn't get that?"

"Yeah. No. It's all about Kyle pretty much. The number one boy. Dad's really into the lineage thing."

Jason put an arm around Darla and pulled her close. "You're number one with me, Squeaker," he said. "Hey, maybe I can get your dad to hire me to actually manage this place. All Kyle would have to do is ride his board and get smoked up all day long. We could move out here and run this whole mountain. Would you like that, Squeaks?"

"No."

"I mean, you've got the whole marketing thing down, which they obviously need. I've got food and bev, and I bet the rest I could figure out. What do you say?"

"No." Darla pushed herself against him. "Don't ask me big stuff like that right now," she said. "Not when I'm feeling like this."

"Okay, Squeaks," Jason said. "Don't worry about it."

Darla sniffed. Jason pushed his nose into Darla's ear and exhaled gently. "Now I'm wide awake," he said.

"Me too."

"You know, you're sort of a moaner yourself under the right conditions."

Darla pushed herself against him, but said nothing.

"Wanna see if we can drown out Ellie and the ski bum?"

"Mmmmm."

"C'mon."

"Mmmmmm. I don't know. I just want to oh fuck FUCK!"

Darla jumped up and stood in the middle of the room, spinning in circles and slapping at her legs and stomach.

"What is it Squeaker? What's wrong?"

"A mouse. A motherfucking MOUSE ran right across my leg."

"You sure?"

"YES I'M SURE. That's probably what ran over the bed before too. While you were still asleep." Darla pulled on a pair of black sweatpants and a grey sweater, not bothering with underwear.

"What are you doing?"

"I'm getting out of here. I've had it with this place."

"You kidding? We just *got* here. And there's like a blizzard going on outside. I don't think there's anywhere else to stay in Sunny Valley but this old lodge."

"I don't care. This place is disgusting. Whatever dad is up to I don't want any part of it. I'm getting out."

The room door slammed, shaking the walls and the deer antler chandelier. Jason exhaled and climbed out of bed. This was not fun, but he knew once Darla decided something, there was no stopping her. Jason dressed himself and began stuffing ski clothes into their matching red suitcases. He was careful to shake each item before packing it, looking for mice. The gaunt face of the gun-toting cowboy on the far wall watched with scowling disapproval.

Downstairs, Darla was in such a hurry to get out of the Lodge that she almost didn't see the tall man standing behind the darkened front desk as she stalked past. She turned to fire a few words at him but then stopped completely. He was very tan and his face, though deeply lined, was thin and handsome. Half his face was smiling, the corner of his mouth lifted

in surprise, but the other half was cold, dead and impartial. For some reason his split expression upset Darla more than everything else. She
turned, threw herself at the heavy wooden lobby door, and pushed out into
the night.

CHAPTER 2

Stephanie Price fell down the mountain. Last night's snow, still powdery, blew around her like moths, like stars. She fell through the top of the run, an old avalanche chute, carving a single exhilarating arc. Just above the tree line Stephanie planted a pole, lifted out of her hips, and shifted her skis by a few millimeters to dodge the huge Jeffrey pine at the base of the chute. Big Red's trunk was scarred by the edges of many skiers who hadn't made the turn. Stephanie herself had racked up against Big Red more than once. In fact Big Red broke her nose when she was ten.

After Big Red came The Gallery, a dense stand of lodgepoles that Mr. Tescher's crew never thinned. You had to lift and shift with just the right rhythm through the trees or you'd Bono for sure. Sometimes you had to simultaneously lift your skis while ducking your head to avoid thick branches. It wasn't a move any ski instructor could teach, which was why flatlanders never came through The Gallery. If they tried the chute at all, they chickened out at Big Red and turned north to traverse over to one of the groomed runs.

On crust or ice The Gallery could be heart-in-the-throat terrifying, even for Stephanie. But today, with a six foot base and two feet of snow fresh from last night's storm, it was fun, like flying one of those Star Wars fighter jets through a field of asteroids and bad guys. The lodgepoles spun by. Stephanie lifted, inhaled deep from her belly, and fell down the mountain.

The Gallery ended abruptly at a cornice, The Holler. Up until about four years ago, Stephanie could ski out of the trees and launch right off the edge, catching fifteen feet of air and landing right in front of the chair lift line below. Everyone would whistle and yell until they realized who she was.

But you needed a really good base of snow to cover the boulder pile at the bottom of The Holler and the drought years had barely dusted them. This year was a lot better, but there still wasn't enough base for that particular trick.

Instead of launching off The Holler, Stephanie slowed through her last two turns and stopped at the end of the trees where she could look out over Sunny Valley. The storm had lifted early that morning, leaving blue Sierra skies over the fresh white of new snow. Stephanie moistened her lips and whispered:

> *The night of storms has gone*
> *The sunshine bright and clear*
> *Breathes life into our Valley's dawn*
> *And sparks the winter air*

Stephanie put her hand to her mouth and laughed, a tiny, guilty laugh that barely reached to the nearby pines. "People die," she said aloud. "They die all the time. It's natural."

Straight ahead and three hundred feet down she could see Mr. Tescher's Ski Center, brown against the white. The Ski Center was covered in cedar shingles except for the west wall that had started to buckle last season. Mr. Tescher's crew propped the wall up over summer but they hadn't bothered to re-shingle. Now the ski shop and the rental center were just ugly plywood boxes.

Three lifts rolled up the mountain. From what Stephanie could see they were mostly empty. It was amazing that everyone in the world wouldn't want to be at Sunny Valley today, skiing through fresh powder under blue skies. But four years of drought had scared people off. The good snow this year had brought back only a few of the old customers.

Maybe it was better this way, Stephanie thought. There weren't many jobs, no tips, and no rich flatlanders paying ten or even twelve dollars an hour for someone to ski with their kids. But at the big resorts near Lake Tahoe—where rich flatlanders could easily be found—you couldn't ski all day on untracked snow. A thousand doofuses tracked up the good stuff before you could finish your first run.

Stephanie stretched out her hands toward the scene below. In two months she would turn 21 and Sunny Valley would belong to her. Daddy would drive her down to the courthouse in Pine Butte and they would sign the papers that said so. Stephanie whispered her favorite poem again and laughed quietly. *"This* year," she said. "I want a new poem *this* year."

Below the Ski Center, fifty yards down the narrow road that the county plow was still clearing, was the Lodge. The Lodge was a huge log building Stephanie's father had built after he'd come back from Vietnam. Even from up on the ski mountain Stephanie could see the foundation of the wing that had burned. It was covered unevenly with white, like a broken tooth. The blackened logs on that side of the main lodge were also patched with stained plywood.

Stephanie unstrapped the poles from her hands. She planted one firmly in the snow and took up the other, holding it to her shoulder and sighting along its length as if it were a rifle. She took aim first at the Lodge and then followed the snowy road leading to the ski mountain as if taking a bead on a moving animal. "Pow!" she said. "Pow! Pow! Pow!"

She put her ski poles back on her wrists and, before turning to go, took a glance further along the valley. Another dark log building was hidden in the trees a short way up from the valley floor. A finger of black smoke curled from the chimney. That was Mr. Tescher's house. The visitors were staying there now, the folks from Vermont. Stephanie was supposed to give one of them a lesson today. The daughter. Stephanie smiled a few times, practicing. "Each man kills the thing he loves," she said aloud. She pinched the corners of her mouth with her gloved hands, trying to make her smile bigger. "That's by Oscar Wilde. Do you like Oscar Wilde?"

Stephanie planted a pole and lifted. She let her skis run right along the edge of the cornice. In another hour or two, after the sun had warmed the snow, her weight might be enough to snap the cornice off and send it down the slope in a white avalanche. But Stephanie could feel the tension in the snow under her skis. She knew it was safe.

Stephanie glided along the extreme edge of the cornice for about twenty yards, building speed, before planting, lifting and turning downhill. The edge crumbled a little under her skis and Stephanie was again falling, surrounded by stars of snow. She was falling, but her sideways momentum carried her across the face, far enough to miss the rock pile at the base of The Holler and land halfway onto the groomed section of Nova, the wide blue run down the middle of the mountain that the flatlanders loved.

Stephanie made only one turn on Nova, a clean Giant Slalom carve. She was going so fast at the bottom that her hockey stop showered the lift operators with snow, two of the dark-looking Chileans that Mr. Tescher and Stephanie's dad had hired this year. They worked cheaper than the folks from down in Pine Butte and did what they were told.

The lifties brushed snow out of their hair and off their ski jackets, laughing. "You go fast, miss," said one, the handsome one. "Maybe we race."

Stephanie unstrapped the ski poles from her wrists and shuffled forward to what would have been the start of the lift line if there had been anyone waiting. The lift machinery rattled behind the Chilean boys, an old twin chair that creaked and complained whether there was anyone to pull up the mountain or not.

"Miss…" One of the boys held his hand out, offering to pull her forward into position for the next chair. "I help…"

Stephanie ignored the hand. Instead she unzipped her hood and folded it back. Then she pushed her goggles up onto her forehead and looked at the lift boys, first one and then the other. She didn't blink, didn't smile, but just waited until she was sure they knew who she was.

The younger one, not the cute one, whispered something in Spanish. Then both stepped back and stood aside.

Stephanie boarded the lift. As her skis left the ground she turned in the chair to look back at them. The lifties were standing stiff as soldiers, silent as snowmen. "I want to see you at Karnival," she shouted back at them. The lift cable squeaked through the overhead pulleys. "*Both* of you."

"Yes, miss," the younger one said, feebly.

Stephanie settled back into the creaking chair for the slow ride up the mountain. She looked around again with satisfaction at the Valley coming into view as her chair lifted higher. In two months Daddy would drive her to the courthouse in Pine Butte and they would sign the papers. Then *he* could come back. *He* would come back and write her a new poem.

CHAPTER 3

Kyle's face was pressed hard on the waxing bench, so hard that his front teeth cut into his lip. Blood was in his mouth, he could taste it. There was nothing he could do about it, though, because his arm was twisted way up behind his back. That new guy, Gavin, the guy with the weird mouth, was holding Kyle's wrist in some fancy judo hold. Icicles of pain went up his arm if he moved even an inch.

Kyle tried to say "What the *fuck*?" but only blood came out, red dots soon lost among the million blobs of colored ski wax that covered the bench.

The hot waxer was still running. Kyle could feel its heat near the top of his head. The chemical smell of melting wax floated around him.

"You're not going to do *thet*. You're not ever going to do *thet*, are you?" said the Gavin guy. Something was wrong with his face so he was always talking out of the side of his mouth, like a gangster in an old movie. "Are you going to forgit about it?" he said quietly, right into Kyle's ear, "or am I going to slice your balls off?" His whole body pressed onto Kyle's back, like he wanted to hump him over the wax table. Kyle tried to say "fag" but he couldn't move his jaw. More blood dripped out and now his face was smeared with it.

Gavin fumbled for something, reaching along the tool rack over the bench. A chill ran from Kyle's scalp to his dick when he realized that Gavin was reaching for the shop's base flattener, a sawed-off section of an old ski that had one steel edge ground razor sharp. Three weeks ago—on Kyle's first day at the mountain—he'd slit his thumb on the base flattener while scraping down his own board. The fucking thing was so sharp he didn't even notice the cut until his white turtleneck was pretty much ruined.

Kyle bucked and twisted. His whole world was now the smell of hot wax from the buffer, Gavin's chewing gum breath, and the need to get away from both of them. This crazy fuck really meant to cut Kyle's balls off. With the base flattener.

"Mother *fucker.*" Kyle finally got some words out, but only because Gavin had loosened his hold. A pneumatic hiss signaled that the ski shop door was opening. The base flattener dropped onto the floor. Suddenly Kyle's arm was free and he could push himself off the bench.

"You boys done with your break?" It was Lance, the local who ran the repair shop. He was also captain of the Flying Coyotes, Sunny Valley's ski patrol. Kyle's eyes were full of tears and sweat. At first all he could see was the green blur of Lance's shop apron. He rubbed his shoulder and elbow. "This stupid motherf…"

"Shut up."

"But I'm telling you…"

Without another word the green shop apron filled his vision. Lance hit Kyle full on the side of the head with his open palm, a massive slap that knocked Kyle onto the cold cement.

A pair of clogs crossed the floor. The door opened and hissed: Gavin leaving without a word. Kyle saw more green as Lance bent down into his field of vision. He smelled of cigarette smoke.

"What did you say about her?" Lance said.

Kyle half swallowed a sob, but that was all he could manage. Tears streamed out. "I'm going home," he said.

"Back to Pussyton, Vermont? Sure. Tell all your preppy buddies you couldn't handle it out west? I hear your rich daddy and fairy princess sister got here last night. She ran screaming out of the Lodge in the middle of the night. You pussies should all go back where you came from."

Kyle's head was clearing, the pain in his face and shoulder were fading, but he still couldn't get up. His arms and legs were floppy, like he'd done a bunch of pot and Ecstasy together. He rolled onto his side. The icy floor felt good against his face.

Lance put a hand down. "Where are they all, anyway? Your pussy family. How's your sister? She cute?"

"She's a fucking bitch. They're skiing. Darla's taking a lesson. What the fuck else would they be doing?"

"Your daddy really trying to buy the valley?"

"You just wait."

"What'd you say to Gavin, prep boy?"

"Nada."

"What'd you say about Stephanie Price?"

"I didn't say anything about Stephanie Fucking Price. My dad..."

Lance stood up and drove a kick into Kyle's stomach. It left him airless and gasping.

"I don't care about your dad. I don't care if he's buying this crap hole. Don't lie to me, that's my advice. Tell me what you said."

"How do you know I said anything?" The words squeezed out.

"The fact that you're lying on the floor drooling blood when you and Gavin should be scraping down the rental skis tells me something. I just want to know exactly what it was."

"I just...I just said she was nice."

Another stomach kick, this one with some ribs attached. Kyle rolled over but as far as pain was concerned he was numb.

Lance's blurry face and green apron loomed into view again. More stale cigarette smoke. "Nobody's ever said Stephanie Price was nice. Nobody. So what *did* you say?"

"Nothing. Just that she's got nice tits."

"And what else?"

"And that I was going to ask her out. For Karnival. Get her all into me and stuff."

Lance grabbed Kyle's shoulders and pulled him into a sitting position, his back against the waxing bench. "You going to puke?" he said.

Kyle could only look at him, the green blur. An hour ago Kyle had been cutting moves in the Sunny Valley Monster Pipe. Then he'd actually showed up for work like he was supposed to. This whole resort was going to be his someday. His dad said so. It should be totally great but so far it was some fucked-up world that made no sense.

"Really, prep boy, you going to puke?"

Lance's breath smelled like acid. With the wax machine and the moldy stink of ski boot liners, it was too much. Lance stepped to one side as Kyle leaned over and spewed yellow vomit across the tech room floor.

Lance went to the back of the room and dug through some cupboards. "You may not appreciate it, prep boy, but Gavin was doing you a favor."

"Whatever. He'd better fucking watch out. All you assholes better watch out."

Lance came back with an armful of rags, old cotton towels from the Lodge. He threw them into Kyle's lap. "I'd stay away from her if I were you," he said.

Kyle leaned against the bench. He closed his eyes and shook his head from side to side. His hair caught in a splinter sticking out of the side of the bench. It pulled with a sharp, painful snag. "Fuck," he said. "Why's everyone so fucked up about Stephanie Price? So her dad owns that fucked up old Lodge? So what?"

Lance lit a cigarette. He untied his apron, holding the cigarette so tightly in his teeth that Kyle thought he was going to bite it in two. "She turns 21 next week. If you don't know why you should care about that, I'm not going to tell you," he said. "Ask around. Educate yourself. All I'm going to say is that whenever there's major shit in this valley, Stephanie Price is at the center of the storm."

Lance threw his balled-up apron in Kyle's face. "I gotta get up on the mountain. I got patrol. Get this place cleaned up. The wax bench too and then get those rental skis scraped down."

Searching the floor, Lance stooped and picked up the base flattener from under the bench. Holding it in his right hand, he used the steel edge to shave a few hairs off his left forearm. "I'll resharpen this myself," he said.

CHAPTER 4

She taught me to ski.

My woolen mittens were old, threadless and stained with snot but she held them in her white-gloved hands and skied backwards, guiding me down the bunny slope in my first turns. My skis wedged desperately into the snow, ankles cranked painfully inward, trying to grip the hillside. My legs trembled. Up, she said, and down, first squeezing my left mitten and then the right. It was like she was pumping my heart by hand. Don't look at your skis, she said. Look at *me*. I never looked at my skis again. Stephanie's face was rounder then, or was it the effect of the silver fur-trimmed hood that she wore on the mountain? Her cheeks and nose were always red, either from cold or from laughter. Her eyes were a rich brown, like tree bark, but they lightened on some days, as if a storm had cleared behind them.

Two minutes into that first lesson my skis slipped out from under me and I fell. She reached under my arms and tried to tug me upright, even though I was nine years old, a year older than her and a lot bigger. I really was helpless in the snow, kicking and flailing like the drowning boy I was. But her arms calmed me, centered me, and I stood up. The next day I fell again, but with a purpose. When she reached down to help me up I took her glove and pulled, catching her off balance—not an easy thing to do, even then. She collapsed on top of me in a pile of skis, poles, goggles and gloves. I pushed snow down the back of her parka and she shrieked with anger and then with laughter. She tried to escape, tried to fight back, but finally just lay, panting, on top of me, grinning like a cat. A woman watched us, a tall beautiful woman in white.

I remember more, earlier, though maybe I'm not supposed to. It seems I'm not supposed to know who I am or why I'm alive. I remember a foster home in Los Angeles and five other children. In that home clothes were handed down from the older children to the younger once a year, at Christmas time. There was a chore wheel, one chore per child per day, that kept each of us in a separate part of the house all afternoon, scrubbing tile grout or dusting old magazines or picking weeds from the cracks in the driveway. At bedtime our foster parents walked down the hall, stopping at each bedroom door. We would call out in order, so they would know we were all in bed. I was number six, the youngest, and "six" was the first word I learned to say. It was the first word I learned to write at school.

My daily walk to school crossed an enormous black parking lot, some days so hot that the tar softened underfoot. The sky shrieked above with airplanes landing at the nearby airport. They rained down ash and gasoline and their shadows passed overhead like vultures.

No talking was allowed while we got ready for school in the morning, nor while we did our chores at night. And on those endless walks across the black fields, the hot parking lots blown with garbage, none of us *could* talk. There were no words for what was inside us because there was nothing inside. Years later, in a college prep English class at Pine Butte High School, I wrote a few lines about what I could remember:

> *The darkness has no equal*
> *The emptiness a curse*
> *There is no more salvation*
> *On this cold and rotting Earth*

I tried to write words that would free what was imprisoned inside me. But, as I've since learned, it was already too late. I've been trapped in this cold and rotting Earth since I was born.

I still don't know what gods lifted me from those soulless flat places and took me, at age nine, to a winter landscape such as I had only seen in children's books, in images so strange from my experience that there was no reason to believe that snow and sky and mountains and trees really existed. Instead of blacktop there was white—a sometimes painful white when the full Sierra sun was out and I'd lost my sunglasses again. Instead of endless flat miles of oily streets, of burning sidewalk, of weed-filled backyards, there were mountains. Clean granite domes or raw volcanic crests. There were real birds instead of chemical ones—red tailed hawks, osprey and eagles. And instead of the blank, loveless faces of my foster parents, there was Bucky Price and the tall woman in white. Instead of hard gray step brothers and sisters, there were Thad and Stephanie.

I entered my first ski race the next season. Bucky thought it was a hoot—the flatlander kid in his castoff clothes (reluctant gifts from Thad)—against the locals, boys who had been born on skis, with the icy Sierra streams running in their veins. I had old skis and no technique whatsoever. I turned with my ass, the way all the other flatlanders did on their ski weekends, and flailed my arms like a dying monkey.

But I finished third and earned some respect. The locals have mountains in their blood. I have something else.

On the awards stand for the nine-to-twelve year olds, it was Stephanie Price who put the medals around our necks. I bent down to take my bronze medal and when she kissed me she pushed her tongue into my mouth. I grabbed the fur lining of her parka and pulled, trying to crush whatever was between us into nothingness, trying to pull her as close as I possibly could.

CHAPTER 5

"Look out, Squeaker!" Jason stopped a few feet from where Darla had fallen. His skis sprayed her with snow, not too much. "You feelin' better today?" he said. "How's the lesson?"

"I'm *fine*," Darla said. She pushed on her ski poles, trying to get to her feet, but her skis kept sliding out from under her. "Only it's like I've never skied before in my *life*. Did you see my instructor up there? That Stephanie girl?"

"No. What's she look like?"

"I've *got* to get up before she comes back."

"You want a hand, Squeaks?"

"NO! This is so embarrassing. She's changed my whole skiing style and now I'm totally confused. I swear I can't make a single turn anymore without falling on my face. Where's dad?"

"He took a different trail down. I'm supposed to meet him at the lift."

"Thank god. He would really think I'm a dope if he saw me on my butt like this." Darla kicked her skis in and pushed on her poles but then sank back into the snow with a sigh. "Now I'm exhausted," she said. "And I've only done one run!"

"You sure you don't want a hand up?"

"NO! And stop asking."

Jason looked up at the sky. He shrugged off his jacket and tied it around his waist. "What a day," he said. "Can you believe this place? It's like we're in Hawaii but there's eight feet of snow on the ground. And no lift lines! I'm going to ski myself dead if I'm not careful."

Darla grunted and finally managed to get to her feet. "I'm glad you're having so much fun," she said. She scanned the broad, open slope around them, staring uneasily at the line of pines that defined the edge of the trail. She shivered involuntarily. "It's so *empty* here," Darla said. "I've hardly seen anyone all morning. I don't like being out here by myself."

"I think it's awesome," Jason said. "For once I can ski as fast as I want without having to dodge a bunch of slow boats."

Darla looked back at the tree line and then up the slope toward the exposed rocky ridge at the top. Where was her instructor? This Stephanie girl was supposed to be some famous Olympic skier but the lesson so far had been a disaster and now she'd disappeared. Of all the ski resorts in the world, why had Darla's dad picked this weirdo place?

"Squeaks? You okay?"

"Huh?"

"Something wrong?"

"No. Nah. I just remembered something, that's all. I figured it out." Darla looked up the empty slope. An icy pit formed in her stomach, a familiar hollow. "I don't know what's wrong with me," she said. "I'm worse than usual."

"Don't say that Squeaks."

"No, really. I'm sorry about last night. I really am. You were being so sweet and I was just such a pitiful, helpless blob."

"Well…"

"And then I went all Amazon on you. I know, Jase. I'm sorry. I mean, we could have been totally killed out there in the snow. I don't know what I'm going to do about myself. Take some drugs or something."

"Don't say that, Squeaks. Maybe it's just having your Dad and Kyle around."

Darla shook herself vigorously. "Rrrrrgh. I'm okay Jason. You go ski. Go ski fast and have a great time."

"Okay," Jason said. He shuffled his skis and drew closer to Darla. "Do you remember what we talked about last night? About coming out here and all?"

"Um, yeah. A little," Darla said. "I'm thinking about it. A little."

Jason planted a loud kiss on her sunburnt cheek. "Thanks, Squeaks. That's all I ask."

A skier appeared on the rise, a Ski Patroller in a red jacket. He was moving quickly but passed very close to Darla and Jason, turning around them as if they were a slalom pole. He passed close enough that Darla could see his face, deeply tanned and worn. He had a cigarette in his mouth. Snow splashed against Darla's legs.

"Who's that jerk?" Jason said.

Darla looked down, tapping her ski pole onto the snow. She closed her eyes. Live *here*? In this white emptiness? She pictured the strange handsome man at the Lodge front desk last night. Like the Ski Patroller who just passed, his worn face seemed to tell of some deep pain. Darla shivered, but then jammed her ski pole hard into the snow. She was just being a baby again, blubbery and weak. And here Jason was deciding their lives for them just like that!

"'Bye, Squeaker!" Jason said. "I'll see you at the Ski Center after the lifts close. We'll get a hot dog or something."

Darla lifted a gloved hand to wave goodbye but he was gone. Stephanie Price, Darla's instructor, appeared in the next breath, arriving in near silence and stopping lightly beside Darla.

"Where have *you* been?" Darla said.

"I thought I'd let you ski this run by yourself and let you get a feel for the mountain." Stephanie said. She smiled, a stiff, wooden smile as if she had to force herself. "Some people ski better when the instructor isn't watching. Did you know that?"

"No, I didn't know that."

"Did you try the exercise with your poles?"

"I did," Darla said. "I felt the mountain all right. I almost broke my neck." Darla took a deep breath. "I know I look like a complete klutz," she said, "but really I've been skiing a lot. I mean, my Dad *owns* a ski area in Vermont."

"I understand," Stephanie said in her funny, stiff voice. "But sometimes even the pros pick up bad habits. Are we ready to give it another try?"

Darla wasn't ready. She was on her feet and more or less put back together after her yard-sale crash, but she still needed a minute, a little more time to explore this super-deja-vu sensation she was having right now.

"My mother loved this run," Stephanie said. "It's an easy slope but the view is quite nice. She would take it real slow and just carve out the most beautiful turns you ever saw."

Darla's mouth fell open. "I was…I was just thinking about *my* mother," Darla said, feeling a little breathless.

"You mother couldn't come out with you guys?"

"She passed away," Darla said. "When I was little." Darla was biting her lip so hard she was sure it was going to start bleeding. "This place has got me thinking about her, though, for some reason."

"I'm very sorry," Stephanie said. "My ma is buried up there on Little Spring Ridge." Stephanie pointed with her ski pole to the far side of the valley. "You couldn't ask for a more peaceful place. This was her valley, so now she can see it all really well."

Darla was completely speechless. Stephanie seemed to have climbed right into her own imagination, her own fears. As Darla watched, a gust of wind kicked up the snow on the distant ridge, creating a momentary cloud of white against the brilliant blue of the Sierra ski. "I'm…I'm sorry," Darla said. She shook her head, trying to clear it.

Stephanie stepped back and resumed her mechanical smile, then looked up at the sky as if judging the angle of the sun. "Let's try that exercise again, okay?"

"Um, I'm not sure it's really helping."

"Don't worry," Stephanie said, "you'll feel it pretty soon. Let me take your poles. Okay, now hold your hands out in front of you like you're carrying a tray."

Darla did so. She was feeling *something*, anyway. No longer was she blubbery and afraid. Now she just felt perplexed and a little annoyed.

Stephanie lay Darla's ski poles across her extended arms and balanced them carefully. "Okay. I'll ski down a few turns and then stop. You just ski straight towards me. Keep your shoulders calm and steady so the poles don't fall off."

"I'll try it, but…"

"And close your eyes."

"Huh?"

"Close your eyes. You'll be surprised how much it helps. You'll really feel the mountain that way."

"How can I ski toward you if my eyes are closed? What if I hit some-one?"

"You'll be okay. Just try. Just get a real good feel."

Stephanie swished away down the slope. Darla took a breath and closed her eyes. Of all the stupid ideas. She really was going to break her neck now. Fortunately this ski area was so seedy and broken down that there was no one to run into. She held her arms in front of her with the ski poles precariously balanced and began her run.

Which almost ended on the very first turn. As her speed picked up, Darla tried to turn but felt the poles in her arms tipping. She wobbled and nearly caught an edge but then settled down again and found her balance. She was going faster, though, and could feel the cold air passing around her ears along with the hot Sierra sun on her forehead.

She *had* to turn now or she was going to crash. Slowly, so as not to tip the ski poles balancing on her arms, Darla dipped her knees and pushed her shins against the front cuffs of her boots. She *could* feel some-thing. A change, a change in her relationship with the snow, the slope. She dipped deeper, pushed harder, and felt her skis flex and bend. They came around into such a nice round turn that Darla almost dropped her poles in surprise. She straightened and felt her skis line back up below her.

A skier passed, rocketing by, someone laughing with a demonic cack-le. Was he laughing at her? Darla didn't care. After an afternoon of frus-tration she was finally feeling it, that nice round carving turn where the mountain seemed to be doing all the work. She dipped and straightened, dipped and straightened, focusing on the sensation of snow under her skis, feeling each grain as the skis transitioned from edge to flat to edge. Each turn put new energy into her legs, a little whoop! in her belly. Maybe this was what Stephanie's mom felt, doing this same run over and over again. Darla stopped at the next turn, gasping. She'd been holding her breath practically the whole run. She opened her eyes and found Stephanie standing beside her.

"That was better," Stephanie said.

Darla blinked, surprised at the snow and sky around her. "Well, yeah," she said. "I think I kind of got it. Felt it. What you were talking about."

"Oh good. There's a lot of power in this mountain, if you can learn how to use it."

Darla blinked again. She was beginning to think Stephanie was a good instructor, but she said some weird stuff, no doubt about it.

"Let's just ski the rest of the run," Stephanie said. "You don't have to balance your poles. But you can close your eyes if you want to."

"I might," Darla said. She was definitely ready to ski again, to feel what she'd felt before. She took a deep breath. "I'm...I'm *sorry* about your mom."

Stephanie pointed herself down the slope but then turned back. "Isn't this nice?" she said. "Imagine if you lived here. We could ski together every day."

Stephanie released and flew down the slope, leaving Darla standing open-mouthed. Those were exactly Jason's words, as if she'd overheard them. But Stephanie had been nowhere in sight.

Darla shook her head and strapped her poles back onto her hands. She would ski and ski well. She would not be weirded out by darkness or snow or dead moms or demons under the bed or anything else. She pushed herself forward and felt her speed build. The faster she went, she knew, the more she would feel it, the magic of the mountain, the whoop! Darla closed her eyes and skied.

Chapter 6

Wallace Collins looked up into the dim rafters of the cabin. The construction here was very much like the Lodge. Huge logs, darkened by time and fireplace smoke, made up the walls, supporting posts and beams. The wood was beautiful but made the room feel heavy and oppressive. There was only one window, which was in the eastern wall overlooking the valley.

What a waste, thought Collins. There were probably excellent views in every direction but here we are cooped up in the dark. Cathedral windows would cost money and change the character of this old log house but they would be worth the money, he thought. The cabin could rent for thousands during high season. Collins made a mental note to get an estimate for some new windows as soon as possible.

"Your house reminds me of Price's Lodge," Collins said aloud, trying to sound agreeable. He was finding his host, Nate Tescher, a difficult man to warm to. "Was it built at the same time?"

Nate Tescher stirred in the deep leather chair near the fireplace. He pushed his hand down the front of his jeans and scratched himself. "Huh," he said, clearing his throat. "Older. Fifty years older. It was build before Price ever showed his face in this valley. My father built it, old Igmar. He wanted our whole clan here but my mother's folks stayed in their stinking shack on the valley floor. They hated old Igmar."

"What shack? I don't recall seeing…"

"An old log cabin. It's gone now. Price bulldozed it to build the Lodge."

Collins laughed. "I can see why he's having trouble with his business. Poor instincts. I would have kept it, fixed it up. Tourists love all that old history."

"When Bucky Price didn't like something," Tescher said, "he crushed it. Rolled over it like a one-man army. Things are a little different now, of course. He's starting to figure out there's bigger things out there, bigger than him."

Nate Tescher cleared his throat again. Collins winced. It was like listening to gravel being shoveled. "Where's that girl of yours anyway?" Tescher said. "The one that walked right out of Price's stinking Lodge and into the storm?"

Collins exhaled loudly. "I am embarrassed about that," he said. I was asleep in my own room, of course, so I could do nothing to prevent it. Darla has always been a foolish, headstrong girl. She's been in her own world, really since her mother died. She's very lucky you drove by last night when you did."

"Huh *huh*. You have no idea how lucky," Tescher said. "Some girl appears right out of the snow in the middle of the night? Around here that's not a good thing. I was scared to death. I nearly turned my Jeep around and drove back down to Pine Butte. Then I saw the husband with the suitcases. Huh *huh*. Jason or whatever his name is. What a jackass."

"That's my son-in-law Tescher. He and my son Kyle may be running Sunny Valley sometime soon."

"Sorry. Your girl's cute though. All that black hair. When I drove them up last night she was soaking wet and mad like you wouldn't believe. It got me thinking…"

"Darla. You're speaking of my daughter Darla."

"Oh yeah. Sure." Tescher scratched himself again. "Where is everyone anyway? They hit the slopes today? It's nearly dark. We should get our business done."

"I believe Darla took a lesson this afternoon and then they were going to have something to eat at the Ski Center before coming back here. We don't want to abuse your hospitality, Tescher."

"She get a lesson with Stephanie? Stephanie Price?"

"Yes."

Tescher fell silent, his face dark. Wallace Collins chattered nervously. "It was good of you to take them in last night," he said. "I'll stay here too, if you don't mind…"

"I taught her everything," Tescher said. His voice was unusually quiet. "She'll tell you the fucking mountain taught her to ski or some magical crap like that. *I* taught her."

"… I slept poorly at Price's Lodge last night. Very poorly. Jason's family left today. They were unhappy with the Lodge as well. They're driving to Tahoe. Of course I'll have to offer to pay for the rest of their vacation." Collins shook his head slowly. "I hope it doesn't further sour relations with Price."

"Huh *huh*. I tried to warn you. You could have all stayed at my place—" he swept his hand toward the thick beams overhead—" at least until Karnival."

"You were right of course. I had no idea the Lodge was so far gone. I thought bringing Price some business would help me get in his good books."

Tescher covered one nostril with his thumb and blew his nose into the fireplace. "Price has no good books," he said. "There's only one book. That's the one where he owns the Valley and the rest of us are rotting underground."

Collins clasped and unclasped his hands. He and Nate Tescher had been negotiating for months by telephone over the sale of the Ski Center, but he was still not sure how to talk to Tescher, what kind of man he was. "I'm glad we came, though," Collins said. "The Valley itself is beautiful. This is my first time in the Sierras, in the West. There's a raw, romantic quality here that I've not encountered before. It's just as I'd heard." He drew in a breath.

> *The night of storms has gone*
> *he sunshine bright and clear*
> *Gives glory to our Valley's dawn*
> *And sparks the winter air*

"Shut up."

The room fell silent. Tescher crossed to the window on the east side of the room. "Huh *huh*. He's got that Lodge lit up tonight," he said.

"Who has?"

"Price. Come look."

At the window Collins felt the temperature drop a few degrees. The alcohol in Tescher's drink, warmed by his fat hands, floated up. Collins, smelling it, pressed his lips together.

"You'd think the whole Olympic ski team was staying at that lodge tonight. And all their groupies," Tescher said.

A light snow was falling but through it Collins could see the Lodge, just a hundred feet below. It was indeed lit up. Every room light, every exterior flood and spot light, even some multi-colored lights strung unevenly along the roof, perhaps a Christmas leftover, shone brightly. The effect was oddly harsh, a huge log box assaulted with light, the glow magnified by the snow piled around it. Nothing about the scene was homey or welcoming.

"Full occupancy on a Wednesday night?" Collins said. "That's impressive."

"Huh *huh*. That's where he's got you. All those rooms are empty. Since you folk cleared out there's not a soul registered. I know that for a fact. We've got our spies, Collins, eh?"

Wallace Collins blinked. "That can't be," he said.

Snow fell. Collins searched the scene for life. The blinds in every room were flung open, which was odd in itself, but he could see no movement. There were no guests dressing for dinner, no parents putting kids to bed; no one showering and changing after a vigorous day on the slopes. Only light, that strangely harsh, glaring light.

"Is he mad?"

"You tell me. Here I've got the best Ski Center in California and he's got a thirty-room lodge with no guests. *And* a hundred acres of land within walking distance of my lifts lying around doing nothing, overgrown with piss fir and Tamarack. Is he crazy? I think I'm crazy to have put up with it for so long. Just give me my money, Collins. Then he's your problem."

Collins made a thin smile. His initial payment on the Ski Center, a certified check for a half million dollars, was folded in his wallet. He almost imagined he could feel the heat of it through his trousers. He and Tescher had shook hands on the deal, and it was a good one, but the thought of handing over so much money pained Collins.

"I think you've made the right decision, Tescher," Collins said, trying to reassure himself. "I know you have a lot of history here, family ties and so forth…"

"You don't know, Collins. You don't know half. *My* people were the first in Sunny Valley. We owned it. It was taken from us. Taken from me."

"So you've said. I'm surprised you could never do anything about it until now, Nate. Surely a fellow like you could've figured out how to get Price out of the way and, ahem, consolidate his property with yours so you could have a *real* resort."

"What do you mean 'a fellow like me.'?" Tescher said. He wheezed loudly.

"I only meant…"

"Oh, I getcha. You're right Collins. We're just cowboys up here. *Huh.* Frontier justice and all that stuff. Well you just think about it. If I haven't strung him up by a lamp post yet there must be a reason. All I've got—all I'm selling—is the Ski Center buildings and my lease on the mountain. A *lease*. It's a hundred year lease, but even if Price has an accident, I've still got a landlord. Get me? And what a landlord."

"Who? Who would hold title?"

"Look, you want Price to sell before the end of the season. Just remember that. We'll do whatever it takes to get them out of that firetrap old lodge. We're agreed on that, right? Whatever we need to do?"

"I agreed on certain things."

"Don't look so pinched up, Collins. Huh *huh*. You got a face on like an old woman. Let's see what happens with Karnival. It's going to be different this year, what with the good season. Folks are coming up again. Let's see what happens. Which reminds me. Our special friend needs some money. For supplies."

"More money, Tescher? I've given you a fortune already."

"It's not for me. It's for our special friend." He pulled a worn and creased sheet of paper from his woolen shirt and handed it to Collins. "Read that," he said. "Our friend wants to meet you tomorrow afternoon. That'll give you time to get down to the bank in Pine Butte and get cash."

"Is this wise? If he and I were to be seen together…"

"Read the note. Huh *huh*. This isn't a shakedown, Collins. We've all got the same goal. It's just operational expenses. I'd cover it if I could, believe me. I'd cover it but I have nothing. Nothing."

Collins read the note and folded it carefully back into its envelope. "This may be unnecessary," he said. "I'm going to talk to Price in person tomorrow. I'll go to the Lodge and lay out my proposal man to man. Then we can avoid all this nonsense."

Tescher started to stand up out of his chair but sank back down again. "We'll see. I wouldn't get my hopes up. It's going to take extreme measures to get Price and his family out of that stinking lodge. But don't worry, you'll get it all, Collins. You'll have your empire. Between Sunny Valley and your place in Vermont, Pusserton…"

"Presserton."

"*Presser*ton. Huh. Presserton. You'll be quite the bicoastal ski king. A mogul. A mogul of moguls. Get it? Huh *huh*."

Wallace Collins's arms were straight at his sides, his fingers working open and closed. "It's not final yet, Nate. You've got my deposit—a half million dollars!—but you don't get the rest until I have Price's signature on the deed to the Lodge."

"Huh *huh*. You'll get it. Wait 'til Karnival, Collins. Wait 'til Karnival."

Collins pressed his hands against his temples. "You said if Price passed away I would still have a landlord. I presume you mean his son, Thad."

"Huh. I wish. Thad I could handle. Nope. Title passes to Stephanie Price, bitch goddess of the Central Sierra. Stephanie who turns twenty one in April."

"Twenty one? Meaning she'll come into her inheritance? She'll own the valley?"

"Yes," Tescher said, "Yes she will." A door slammed downstairs. Voices came up from the foyer below: Darla and Jason returning from the day's skiing. Tescher stood up, scratching himself again. "She will," he said, "If she lives that long."

CHAPTER 7

Kyle ran a gloved hand over the metal pole between him and Alejandro. "Shit's *rusty*," he said. "How come nobody's been killed on this fucking lift?"

Alejandro sat in the partner chair and said nothing. He carefully searched the trees passing on the north side. Three days of sunshine had shorn them of snow.

"And *slow*. I'm gonna get my dad to swap this piece of shit with a detachable quad first thing. Still—" he leaned back in the chair and rubbed his eyes—"may as well enjoy the trip. You going to spark up or what?"

"Eh?"

"Spark it up. My back is fucking killing me." Kyle handed over a windproof lighter.

"You hurt your back? Crash and burn?"

"Not me. That new fuck Gavin. He crashed and burned me. I'm going to get that fuck." He rubbed his eyes again. "Shit it's bright. I'm getting a headache."

"You don't wear glasses?"

"Yeah I wear fucking sunglasses. I just left mine in the bunkhouse. Shut up and smoke."

Alejandro pulled a ziplock bag from the chest pocket of his jacket and extracted a half-smoked joint. He lit it with two scrapes of the lighter and inhaled noisily. When his lungs were full he passed the joint to Kyle.

"Fuck yeah." Kyle inhaled, put his hand against the center bar and twisted. "That's better," he said, in gasps. "That's a lot fuckin' better. I could hardly land anything today with my back so fucked up." Kyle exhaled loudly. "Still I totally stuck that Half Double. Did you see me? Bottom half of the pipe? It was sick."

Alejandro took the joint back and inhaled another massive hit. "Your sister?" he said, pointing down. They were passing over the main groomed intermediate run. Darla was skiing slowly down the center, carving round symmetrical turns with her skis. She was concentrating hard on each turn and didn't notice Kyle overhead.

"Yeah. Look how slow she's going. She can't ski for shit. I don't know why she even fucking came except maybe she thinks she's going to horn in on the action."

"There is action?"

Kyle leaned back and closed his eyes. "Dad's buying this place for *me*," he said. "You're going to be working for me pretty soon, Allie. What do you think of that?"

Alejandro didn't reply but continued to watch the trees. The lift was rising now to the steeper part of the mountain.

"There she is," he said.

"Who?"

"Look. In the canyon."

The west side of the lift wasn't a ski run but a granite wound, a ravine running down the center of the mountain. The sides were steep and the bottom full of boulders, punctuated by juniper trees bent and twisted by snow. The canyon was out of bounds to Sunny Valley skiers and snowboarders but despite the screen of trees beside the lift run, Alejandro and Kyle could clearly see the flash of a silver jacket flying, it seemed, through the granite.

"It's her," Alejandro said.

"Of course *she* gets to ski in there. Anyone else would get their fucking pass yanked." Kyle rubbed his eyes.

"Her mother own all this place," Alejandro said, "before she die."

"Yeah, well I'm going to get it now. Maybe her too. She can be my little bitch."

"You like her? Don't look at her too much. She talk to me every day and now I'm scared"

"Where's the doobie?"

"Gone. All gone."

"Shit." Kyle twisted in his seat. "Why does everyone have such a bug up their ass about Stephanie Price anyway? I mean, she made some Olympic team and her dad owns the Lodge, but so what? You'd think she was radio fucking active. I bet she likes a good pop just like anyone else. May as well be me. That Gavin fuck was just trying to scare me off. Wait'll I get him."

Alejandro leaned back to get a last look at Stephanie before she passed out of sight. He sighed loudly. "You don't know?" he said.

"No I don't fucking know. Whatever it is I'm supposed to know I don't know, okay?"

"Her dad. Mister Price. He kill her boyfriends."

"Huh?"

The uphill lift house came into view, a wood shack buried in snow with a gap dug out so the lift operator could watch skiers unload. Peter Kirch, one of the long time locals, stuck a bare hand out the window and waved. Alejandro waved back but Kyle didn't.

"What do you mean he kills her boyfriends?"

"With a knife. Very sharp knife." Alejandro smiled and drew a finger over his neck. "You fock her, you fock you."

Alejandro turned in his seat and lined up his snowboard to dismount from the chair. His snowboard hit the snowy ramp and Alejandro stood up. With a flick he tossed his long black hair behind him, waved again to Peter in the lift house, and was gone.

Kyle should have done the same. Traditional ski lifts are not designed for snowboarders. A skier need only stand up and glide forward but snowboarders ride the lift facing the wrong way. Kyle, startled by Alejandro's description, didn't notice that they were at the top of the lift until it was almost too late. He jumped off the chair without lining up his board parallel to his forward motion. The front edge caught the ramp, flinging Kyle face down into the snow. Bald laughter rolled out of the lift house, followed by a half-eaten apple that hit Kyle on the head.

CHAPTER 8

Darla took a deep breath, filling her lungs with the morning air. "So *then*," she said, "this poor kid winds up preggers. I mean, she didn't *want* to come to Jason's frat party, it was, like, my idea. She wasn't even *looking* to hook up with anyone. The guy wears a rubber and everything but boom! she got it. I mean, is that bad luck, or what?"

There was only silence in reply, only the creaking of the chair lift as Darla and Stephanie were carried up the slope. Suddenly there was a whooshing sound over head. Darla looked up. Two huge crows wheeled in the sky above them, fighting in the air. Darla looked back at Stephanie who was staring straight ahead.

Darla knew she'd been running off at the mouth since they'd got on the chair lift but she didn't know what to do about it. Her father had pulled Darla aside last night shortly after she and Jason had come back to Mr. Tescher's cabin. He told her to try to make friends with Stephanie. "It will make everything much simpler if they feel they can trust us," he'd said. In Darla's imagination she could see him rubbing his hands together over the great deal he was going to get for this creepy old valley. "I'm hoping we can come to an *amicable* agreement between our two families," he'd said. "Anything else would be a personal disappointment to me."

Darla didn't know what he meant by 'anything else', nor did she care. This whole ski resort thing had little to do with her. Dad was doing it for Kyle, she knew, investing a huge amount so Kyle could have his own playpen. She wasn't sure she wanted Jason involved either. But, still, this morning when she saw Stephanie about to get on the lower lift, Darla hurried to join her. There *was* something special about Stephanie, Darla thought, though she had no idea what it could be. They didn't have a lesson scheduled today, but the long ride on Sunny Valley's incredibly slow lower lift would give them a chance to talk.

Stephanie hiccupped suddenly. She put a gloved hand to her mouth and said "excuse me," and nothing more.

Darla felt herself turning red with embarrassment. She didn't get along with other girls when she was young, but she'd kind of gotten the hang of it when she started at Bennington. The idea was not to expect too much. Talk about hair and sex and leave it at that.

The lift chair passed over the broad main run at the center of the mountain. Few people were on it, but a single ski patroller stood near the top, smoking a cigarette. He glared at a clutch of beginning skiers learning to snow plow a few yards below him. As Darla watched, he flicked his cigarette butt towards the group, planted a pole and then disappeared into the trees at the edge of the slope.

Darla snuck a look out of the corner of her eye toward Stephanie. The girl was mighty strange, but when Darla learned that Stephanie had also lost her mother when she was young, Darla had felt something for her. The girl seemed trapped inside herself. Hardly anything she did or said seemed natural or genuine. Was it from growing up in this remote place surrounded on weekends by loutish snowboarders and ski patrollers? Was it from the loss of her mother? Or something else that had happened to her?

They were halfway up the mountain now. Darla had just resolved not to say anything else--her dad could make friends with Stephanie himself if it was so important--when Stephanie suddenly spoke up.

"Was it a girl?" she said.

"*Huh*?" Darla turned. She had no idea what Stephanie was talking about.

"Your friend who got pregnant. Was her baby a girl?"

Darla looked at Stephanie. She had *actually* been listening! Some of the robot quality had gone out of her face and she looked genuinely interested. "You know what? I don't remember," Darla said. "I'm pretty sure she had the baby, but then her family moved."

Stephanie leaned forward. "And she wasn't married? She had a baby and she wasn't married?"

"Hmm, yeah." Stephanie was changing before her eyes. A few minutes ago she was the ice princess. Now she was like a ten year old girl who didn't know the birds from the bees. "Happens all the time," Darla said warily. "There's no law says you have to be married."

Stephanie sat silent again, as if chewing on this new information.

"There was this other time…" Darla thought she'd follow up with another story from her Bennington days but Stephanie interrupted.

"Do you have any dinner plans?" she said.

"What?"

"Dinner plans. Would you like to join me for dinner tonight? At the Lodge? I think it would be fun."

Darla opened her mouth and closed it again. "Yeah, I guess so," she said. Maybe she *was* getting through.

"That's wonderful. Six o'clock, then. Just come to the dining room."

"I will. That will be…fun."

Stephanie said nothing in response. They sat in silence for the rest of the long, slow ride up the mountain. Darla chewed on her lower lip until she could taste blood.

Chapter 9

Wallace Collins stepped through the Lodge entry and stopped. After walking from Tesher's through dazzling sunlight, the darkness inside the Lodge was paralyzing. He put his hands out and touched the massive log door, a blind man feeling his way.

"Hello?" He called into the dark. Last night this place had been lit up. It had blazed like a bonfire in the middle of the dark valley. Now, today, in near blinding Sierra sunshine, the Lodge was cold and dark as a tomb. Collins took a cautious step forward, waiting for his eyes to adjust. "Mr. Price?"

A few cars passed through the big parking lot outside, heading for the Ski Center. Folks from close by, Collins thought. Nobody's going to travel very far to come to this place if there's no where decent to stay, so they're not getting the wealthy folks from the big cities. No wonder Tescher was so unhappy with Price. Collins took a deep breath and inhaled air from the dark space in front of him. The smell was of age and disuse but it wasn't just dust and stale air. There was a whiff of something organic, something rotting.

"Price?" He took a few steps inside. The front desk, just to the right, was surprisingly tidy. An old-fashioned brass cash register stood on the counter where a small reading lamp lit a guest book and pen. A rustic wood panel with hooks held thirty room keys. No keys were missing, Collins noted. A shotgun leaned on the far wall behind the desk. Another antique, Collins supposed, though it appeared to be newly polished and oiled.

Just behind the desk, mounted on the log wall, was an old photograph enlarged to almost poster size. Collins squinted forward. The photograph was of a man and woman standing together in deep snow. The man was a trapper, perhaps, from the Gold Rush days. He held a rifle in one hand and in the other a string of bloody furs. He had a prominent beak-like nose and was so thin that his clothes looked ready to slide off. His eyes seemed to be light in color but it was hard to tell. As in so many old photographs, the eyes were blurred and obscure.

The girl—she was just a girl, barely coming to the man's shoulder—looked Indian. She had long straight hair and wore some sort of skin robe sewn with beads. She looked healthier than the man and, also unlike him, her coal black eyes were perfectly in focus. She looked at the camera with open hostility.

Collins looked away from the photograph and shivered. He must remember to compliment Price on his interior decorating, his attempt to enhance the rustic atmosphere of the Lodge with historic artifacts, though Collins himself would have chosen something other than that frightening old picture to greet his guests.

A sound came down the hallway from the main room. A repetitive sound, someone chanting or counting. Collins swallowed, took a deep breath, and put one hand onto the rough logs along the hallway, letting them lead him through the gloom.

"Price?"

A fire was burning in the large stone fireplace in the main room. Bucky Price, in jeans and a red lumberjack shirt, was on his knees in front of the fire, his face colored an unearthly orange by the flames.

"C'mon son," Price said. "Do 'em with me."

A large winged chair faced the fire. The back was to Collins, but he could see a black shape twist uncomfortably in it. "That's okay, Dad," said a voice, a thin voice.

"Just twenty, Thad. Do 'em with me. Twenty."

Thad Price exhaled and shifted position. As he did something on his belt caught the fabric of the chair. He twisted, grimacing, until it ripped free. Thad reached behind himself and tore most of the chair covering away, exposing the stained white liner underneath. He looked up and saw Wallace Collins.

"Look who's back," he said. "Back for another quality resort experience." He tied the fabric scrap into a knot and, with a wrist flick, threw it into the fire.

"Mr. Price, Thad," Wallace Collins said. "I hope I'm not intruding. My family skis today so I thought…"

Ignoring Collins, Price held a hand out toward his son. "You want to be in top form to race at Karnival," he said. "You know it. Upper body, lower body, everything. Now c'mon. Gimme ten at least. I'll count 'em out."

Price snapped out ten quick pushups while they watched. The firelight threw his shadow across the floor, so that on the far wall of the Cathedral Lounge some kind of monster lumbered up and down.

"Dad," Thad said.

"See son? I'm not even panting. Now if you and I were to take on a daily program of…"

"DAD. Wake up. We got company."

Price stopped and slowly got to his feet. He looked back into the darkness of the big open room as if searching a dense forest. "Who?" he said. "Who is it?"

Collins came forward into the glow of the fire. "Wallace Collins," he said, holding out his hand. Price looked at it and reached out to shake, moving slowly as if retrieving a difficult memory. Collins nearly leapt back: Price's hand was as cold as death.

"Good to meet you," Price said. "Welcome to Sunny Valley. Is your luggage in the lobby? I'll have…"

Collins coughed into his hand. "To be perfectly honest Price, my family arrived here the night before last. We stayed one night in your beautiful Lodge, but my daughter wanted to sample the other accommodations in the area."

A harsh laugh came from the chair near the fire. Collins turned and now could see Thad in the light. He looked small in the large chair. His pale hair was mussed as if he'd just got out of bed, but the thin strands that fell across his forehead did not hide the deep black eyes beneath.

"Where's that guy?" Thad said.

"Who?" Collins turned and looked behind himself.

"Dad, where's that beaner you hired?"

"Alejandro? He's Chilean, son."

"ALEHANDRO. Where are you, you lazy beaner?"

"I'm sure he's looking after some customers."

"Bullshit. There are no customers. They all run away screaming just like this guy and his family." Thad pointed a thumb at Collins. "I heard all about it yesterday from the beaner." He stopped and with visible effort took a deep breath. "ALEHANDRO. DOS MARTINIS POR FAVOR."

"Two martinis, son? Isn't it a little early in the day for that? Who's the other one for? I'm not sure our friend here is ready for a martini."

"It's for me," Thad said.

Collins clasped his hands together. "Perhaps this isn't the best time for us to discuss business," he said. "I might just…"

"What business?" said Thad. Bucky Price only looked into the fire.

"I've written to your father several times over the summer," Collins said, trying to sound earnest and trustworthy. "I received no response. I know mail service can be unreliable in the mountains, so I thought…"

"*What business?*"

"I own a modest ski resort in Vermont. We've had some good years so I want to re-invest in our industry. There are few opportunities for development in New England so when I heard about Sunny Valley, I was inspired to try my fortunes in the Sierra. 'Glory to the Valley's dawn' and so forth."

"*What?*" Thad said, struggling to sit up in the arm chair.

Price too turned around. "What did you say?"

"It's such a lovely poem." Collins held out his hands. "It makes me think of the Psalms. You see…"

Steps sounded in the dark hallway leading into the lounge. Thad sat up, pleased that his drink was arriving so soon, but then slumped back again. "It's you," he said.

"Daddy?"

"Stephanie sweetheart." Bucky Price turned from the fire, his arms folded.

"I've got an announcement to make. I'm glad you're here too, Thad. You'll want to hear it."

Thad snorted.

"Perhaps I really should come back later," Collins said. He took a step backward.

Stephanie turned to him. "You're Mr. Collins, aren't you?" she said. "Darla's father."

"Yes Miss Price."

Stephanie held out a hand and Collins shook it. Unlike her father's hand, Stephanie's was hot.

"We had such a fun lesson yesterday. She has very good balance for a seasonal skier. I hope you encourage her. She could be a competitive bracket skier in a few years."

"Thank you, Miss Price. My son Kyle is really the star of the family. Have you met him? He arrived in Sunny Valley last month to help Tescher with his operation."

"Sweetheart! Come do some pushups with Daddy."

"I don't want to do pushups right now, Daddy. I've got an announcement."

"Fine, sweetheart. How 'bout you stand on Daddy's back while he does a few?"

Stephanie kicked off her fleece boots and walked across the lounge to the fire, where her father was propped, stiff as a lodgepole, in pushup position. Thad rolled his eyes upward, searching the dark heights of the room.

"Actually…" Collins said, clearing his throat.

"Ready?"

"Daddy's ready, sweetheart."

Stephanie put a foot in the middle of his back and then stepped up lightly, balancing just between his shoulder blades.

"Okay," she said.

Bucky Price lowered himself slowly until his nose touched the flagstones and then with a steady motion pushed back up again. "ONE" he said, and lowered again.

"So what's the big announcement?" Thad said. "Getting a leg amputated?"

"TWO."

Stephanie waited until her father was at the top of his pushup. "I'm going to have a baby," she said.

Bucky Price's chest hit the flagstones with an audible thud. Stephanie didn't lose her balance from the sudden motion but instead hopped gracefully off her father's back. Thad exploded with laughter, pounding the arms of his chair and stamping his feet. He was wiping his eyes when Alejandro arrived out of the gloom to place the martinis on a side table. Thad downed one, coughed, and slapped his leg.

"That's good, Steph. That's excellent."

"It's true, though."

Bucky was up on his feet, his face red. He walked in a circle in front of the fire coughing and hacking, trying to get his breath. Collins backed away, out of the circle of red light.

"It's not something to joke about, Sweetheart," Bucky said, finally.

"I'm not joking. I'm having a baby. I turn twenty one this year, so I've got to prepare for the future."

Thad looked carefully sideways at his father, who had sunk down onto the granite ledge in front of the fire. His voice was quiet. "Who is it, Sweetheart? Who is the lucky fellow?"

Thad took a deep sip from his second martini. "Lucky."

"No one yet, Daddy. Don't be upset. I'm not pregnant *now*."

"Then what is this nonsense?"

"Karnival. I'm going to get pregnant over Karnival. That seems like a good time, don't you think?"

"Who, Sweetheart. Who?"

"Oh, someone. I just thought you should know as soon as possible. I knew it would make you happy."

Bucky Price sat nearly motionless on the granite, the fire blazing at his back. He rubbed a hand slowly across his chest. "This is exciting news, Sweetheart. I'm looking forward to meeting the fellow you think will make such a good father."

"Dad…"

"Shut up Thad. You hear me Sweetheart?"

"Yes Daddy." Stephanie kissed him on the top of his head. Her father reached out and touched her stomach with two fingers. "You hear me Sweetheart?" he said.

"Hmmm hmmm." She turned to Collins. "Don't you have a son, Mr. Collins? Perhaps he would be a good choice. Do you think Kyle would make a good father?"

Price turned to Collins with a look of hatred, something deeper than he had ever seen before. Collins stumbled backwards, and then turned and moved out of the lounge as quickly as he could. He imagined he could feel the hostile eyes of Bucky Price boring into his back.

Once he was away from the fire, Collins found himself back in the dim hallways of the Lodge. Again, the rough log walls guided him as he stumbled through the darkness.

CHAPTER 10

Thirty rooms. On the day I started high school, they became mine. In each room: scour, dust, vacuum. Change linen. Look for money and dirty magazines left behind by guests. Thirty rooms to clean between the time I got home from school and dinner. Clean them even if they hadn't been slept in the night before, though in those days the Lodge was busy from Thanksgiving onward. If I took too long cleaning, dinner was only what was left for me, which was usually very little. If the rooms weren't cleaned correctly—Buck inspected one at random every night—there was no dinner at all.

Stephanie usually trained after school, but some afternoons she helped me, if rolling and giggling on a bed I had just made could be considered helping. At her worst she would pretend to be a rich flatlander guest, throwing her clothes on the floor while I scrubbed in the bathroom. If I came out she would wrap herself in a towel and make a little scream. "I'm calling *management*," she would say, and skip dangerously into the hallway. My stomach ached—all of me ached--but I knew I couldn't follow.

Stephanie was invisible. She could stand giggling in the hallway in just a bath towel without fear that Bucky would catch her. She could walk into the dining room kitchen at dinner rush, take a bottle of wine off the rack and walk back out again and no one would say a word.

I was not invisible. Bucky never hit me, but his punishments were always physical. "You remember better that way," he'd say, and he was right. I remember hanging for half an hour from his chin-up bar near the garbage cans behind the Lodge. When my arms gave out I was allowed to stand in the snow, but only as long as I could endure it in bare feet. Then it was back up on the bar, fingers burning, shoulder sockets straining. If I dropped a guest's suitcase or forgot to snake a sluggish drain somewhere in the Lodge's ancient plumbing system, I knew to take off my boots and walk outside, straight to the bar.

But Stephanie was always nearby. Some nights she sat on the beds, the thirty beds, and read to me from the blue book where we wrote poetry to each other. She would copy her favorites from English class. I would try to write my own, to put something of myself into the empty places around me. Her high, thin voice would pierce the room, pierce my heart, and echo out into the Lodge, dancing in the hallways. She loved to declaim a poem I wrote in English class in imitation of the florid Victorian style:

> The night of storms has gone
> The sunshine bright and clear
> Gives glory to our Valley's dawn
> And sparks the winter air

The indulgence and romance of poetry were pure Stephanie. Poetry is a stage that barely needs an audience. I, scrubbing tile on my knees, was audience enough for her. I would hear her breathe deeply, the pages rustle, and then the piercing voice again, tearing into my graceless words.

> Cold and wild the wind was blowing
> Keen and clear the heaven above
> But though countless stars were glowing
> Absent was the star of love

She sighed when she read. I scrubbed, dusted, felt the blood pounding through my temples. She longed for something but I could not yet believe that it was me.

Her ache was different from mine. Stephanie's mother—the tall woman in white—died only two months after I'd come to Sunny Valley. All I knew was that it was some type of cancer, swift and merciless. Stephanie acted like she had no loss, no ache, but I knew otherwise. The words tumbled out of our blue book, and each one called for something that was lost.

We kissed. We might lie, she just fifteen, on a freshly made hotel bed, giggling in our underwear. We might touch our tongues and feel a heat that could melt the snow pack. But she wouldn't let me really touch her.

She could push me away with a glance. Her body, the snowy fields of her skin, wasn't ready for my hands, rough with cleanser, with scrub brushes, scarred by ice. I know now that I wasn't ready for her either. We would kiss, share a tiny flame, and then she would turn aside and open the book. A small breath would to tell me to listen now, to calm myself and listen. She would read.

> *I heard it then, you heard it too*
> *And winter sweet it sang to you*
> *But like the shriek of misery*
> *That wild wild music wailed to me*

My ache, my fire, would change under her voice. It would soften, spread, but never die.

Chapter 11

Drive to the end of Highway 6. Wallace Collins squinted at the tattered note he'd received last night from Tescher. It was written in a cramped, tortured hand. *You'll see a trail. Follow it to The Spike.* Collins folded the note back up and put it in his jeans pocket.

He looked around—he was at the end of Highway 6, all right. Just a few feet away the black top of the road disappeared under a wall of snow. Plows had pushed the snow banks back enough to make a turnaround for cars and a few places to park. Trying to act casually, as if he knew what he was doing, Collins lifted the rear door of his rental SUV and opened a cardboard box.

It's amazing, simply amazing, what they are doing with outdoor equipment these days, he thought. Collins took a pair of brand new snowshoes out of the box. They were shiny and red, like Ferrari race cars, and the buckles looked ingenious. He didn't bother with the book of instructions. Snowshoes. He closed and locked the rear gate of his rental SUV and slung a small pack onto his back.

Weekend snowshoers had worn a snow ramp from the edge of the plowed highway up to the top of the snow bank, nearly eight feet above the roadway. Collins climbed the ramp with difficulty at first, sliding backwards until he figured out how to kick the serrated teeth on the bottom of the snowshoes firmly into the snow. At the top of the ramp he stopped to catch his breath and look back. Here was an eight foot snow base and it was only January. Glory to the Valley's early dawn, or whatever that saying was. The Sierra Nevadas truly were incredible. This much snow back in Presserton would have crushed the village.

Collins had read that some resorts in the Sierras stayed open for skiing all the way until Fourth of July weekend! He would start that at Sunny Valley just as soon as he could. Collins imagined girls in bikini tops and Levis shorts blowing kisses from the lifts. He laughed at his own depravity. But it would be wonderful.

Collins turned away from the highway and faced the forest. It was dense, mostly pine, not much different from the higher-elevation forests back home. He took a few experimental steps forward in his snowshoes and was pleased with their lightness. Now this was a sport that could be expanded, he thought. Just the thing for non-skiers and grandparents who don't want to risk their old bones on the slopes. The sky overhead was a perfect blue. With the California sunshine all around, Collins felt like he was going for a stroll on an early spring day. Perhaps Sunny Valley could set up a special snowshoe park of some sort. Fifteen dollars for the day, plus snowshoe rental. Some kind of snack shack with hot chocolate for the kids. There were lots of opportunities out here that Tescher and Price were just not sophisticated enough to recognize.

The woods ahead were dense but Collins followed a gap that probably marked a fire road in the summer. Snowshoers had packed a nice track through the gap. Collins tightened the straps on his backpack and walked forward. *You'll see a trail,* the note had said. *Follow it to The Spike.*

It was darker in the trees, though the sky was blue overhead. Collins turned and looked back the way he'd come, catching a last glimpse of the highway. No one had passed since he'd parked.

Collins took off his jacket after the first quarter mile and tied it around his waist. These race car things on his feet were light and nimble. The last snowshoes he'd worn—as a child, on a family outing to Vermont—had been bulky wooden tennis rackets. But walking in snow, even well-packed snow, was hard work. Sweat built up under his flannel shirt. Maybe I'm not such a great athlete after all, he thought. For the last ten seasons all I've done is ride a chair up and ride my skis back down. I should do more of this. Get out in the backcountry and find some of that un-tracked snow. He pulled at his flannel shirt, feeling the uncomfortable dampness on his back.

He thought about the note in his pocket. *Follow it to The Spike.* What in the world was The Spike? Collins's right foot suddenly punched into the snow past his knee. His momentum pushed him forward but, with his leg buried in the snow, he didn't fall. Instead his knee bent the wrong way. Collins gasped. With painful effort he wrenched his foot out of the hole. The snowshoe had fallen off two steps back. Those damn funny buckles! Collins leaned back, wincing at the sharpness in his knee, and found the snowshoe. He tried to strap it back on but ice had balled up under his boot, making it difficult to even step into it. The ends of the snowshoe straps were icy too. Collins's bare fingers (it was such a sunny day he hadn't bothered to bring gloves) were red and raw by the time he had the straps cinched on again.

The snowshoe fell off twice more in the next hour and each time it was harder to put back on. The complicated rear strap was now so icy that he didn't even bother to secure it but just let it flap like the back of an old bedroom slipper. Walking was laborious since he was now dragging one foot through the snow instead of lifting it, and it was tiring to have to keep fiddling with the snowshoes. Sweat dripped off his nose whenever he bent down to adjust the straps.

Finally Collins reached a clearing, an open field at the base of a ridge. In the middle was a clean granite boulder standing upright. Clearly this was The Spike. Snowshoers had left tracks all around it and he could see spots where people had sat for lunch.

Go straight north from The Spike, the note had read. *Climb the ridge.* Collins looked at his watch. He was moving a lot slower than he expected, but he needed a break. He sat down in the snow and took water out of his pack but instantly became cold. Collins pulled his jacket back on but it didn't help much. His soaked flannel shirt felt like a sheet of ice against his back. Collins shivered, shook himself, and stood back up. He'd better keep moving.

Straight north. He hadn't brought a compass, but the trail he'd been following had seemed to run roughly east-west. So *that* way must be north. There were no snowshoe tracks going in that direction, so Collins started across the virgin snow, lifting his shoes high and punching down with effort. One snowshoe came off after ten steps and again after ten more. Collins was breathing heavily and he had not even reached the trees yet. He looked around and saw someone else's tracks going in *almost* the right direction. They veered a little left of where he was, but surely that didn't matter. A ridge was a ridge, after all. You either climbed it or you didn't. Who cared how you got there?

With effort, Collins punched twenty yards through the snow and caught up with the other track. He still felt cold. He zipped all the zips on his jacket and dug through his pockets hoping to find an old hat or scarf but there were none. Kicking through the fresh snow had made him tired, but had hardly warmed him at all. Once he was back in the trees, Collins knew, he would be colder still.

CHAPTER 12

The snowshoe trail turned downhill after a few yards so Collins turned up toward the trees, hoping to get above them and get some sense of the land. He looked at his watch: it was 3:30, half an hour late for his meeting on the ridge. The snow was thick and uneven in the forest, making progress difficult. The branches were dark and dry, hard to push through, and after what seemed like a very short time Collins's breath had turned harsh in his lungs. He was cold, especially in his hands, but everywhere else too. He wondered if he should just head back, but Collins was worn out. The thought of the long return slog though the forest, dragging the broken snowshoe, chilled him more.

The familiar *whish-whish* of skis on snow came up through the trees. Collins saw a dull blue shape moving below. It drew closer. It was Gavin, sliding toward him on cross country skis.

"Yeh not dead yet?" Gavin said, his face unexpressive.

Collins swallowed, not wanting to show how relieved he was. "Couldn't we have met closer to Sunny Valley? Now I'm going to be late getting back."

"I don't care."

"This all may not be necessary. My daughter is having dinner with Price's daughter tonight. They've become friends, I believe. You know it's really Stephanie who is going to control the Valley. I'm hoping Darla can convince her…"

Gavin spat into the snow. "This isn't where we were to meet. I waited at the ridge hef an hour."

"Your directions were imprecise."

"You're lost. But I could follow the treks of those things—" he gestured at Collins's red snowshoes—"pretty easy. If you were a buck, you'd be dead."

"Can we get out of here?"

"I'll fex the shoe first."

"Fix it?"

Gavin dug into his pack and pulled out a roll of silver duct tape. He wrapped it around Collins's boot and the snowshoe several times before tearing it off with his teeth. "Good you didn't lose that shoe," he said. "You've got that much sense, at least."

"I'm glad you've got that stuff," Collins said. "It was looking like a tiring walk back without a proper snowshoe."

"Always carry it. Broken skis, broken bindings can kill you back here." Gavin dug a wool ski cap out of his jeans pocket. "Put this on and follow me," he said.

Gavin led. Twice Collins was sure they were going the wrong way but he said nothing. He was in no position to comment. They soon arrived at The Spike, standing at the edge of the clearing. Collins stepped out into the remaining rays of the setting sun, already feeling warmer. Gavin stayed in the trees.

"Let's do the business," he growled.

"As I said before, there's a chance that Stephanie…"

"She won't."

"…and I don't see why I have to pay for this. I've given Tescher a half million…"

"Shut up."

Collins slung down his pack and dug out a zip lock bag full of cash. He gave it to Gavin who stuffed it in his jacket.

"You don't want to count it? Why do you need two thousand dollars?"

"Hell is expensive. You best git home. You'll ketch yer death."

There was a silence. Wind stirred over the tree tops. Collins shuddered.

"I won't have you beating my Kyle," he said finally. "He is my son."

"He's an idiot. Runs in the family."

Collins looked around nervously, scanning the edge of the trees in what he hoped was the right direction to get back to his car. "That way, right?"

"Just follow your treks." Gavin worked his pole straps over the thin fleece gloves on his hands. Collins could now see that his blue jacket was thin, torn in many places. Underneath Gavin was wearing only a white tee shirt, but he seemed not to notice the piercing cold brought in by the afternoon wind. Gavin turned to go, to ski back into the woods, but Collins stopped him.

"When will you do it?" he said.

"When I'm ready."

"But when's that?"

"The weekend."

"Karnival?"

"He'll call it thet."

"I don't want anyone hurt."

"No one will be who doesn't deserve it."

Gavin slid away, disappearing into the trees. Collins stepped back, tripped over the tail of his snowshoes, but then recovered. His knee burned. He found his tracks from earlier in the day and started down them, limping out of the dense forest.

CHAPTER 13

Movement caught Darla's eye and she looked up. A spider lowered itself out of the gloom, a tiny glowing spot on a ghostly thread. It dropped another few inches and then stopped about two feet over Stephanie's head. Darla opened her mouth to say something but shut it again. Stephanie was talking and from Darla's experience there was no use in trying to interrupt.

"I'm really glad you decided to stay in Sunny Valley," Stephanie said. "We were just starting to have fun."

"Uh, I'm glad too." Darla wasn't though. She'd rather be almost anywhere than having dinner with Stephanie Price in her creepy old Lodge. But Dad had insisted. I need your help Darla, he'd said in his best car salesman manner. I know *you* can get through to her.

Darla wasn't sure exactly what she was supposed to get through to Stephanie. That they should sell the Lodge? Darla sneaked a look up: the spider was still there, turning on its thread, as if basking in the yellow light reflected from Stephanie's hair. Darla and Stephanie were sitting like lovers at a candle-lit table, but there was no one else in the dining room to relieve the feeling that they were dining in a tomb. This room, Darla remembered, had high cathedral ceilings but they were now lost in the darkness overhead. That spider must have lowered itself for a long time. Why stop now? Maybe it was out of thread. Or maybe, like everyone else in Sunny Valley, it was in awe of Stephanie Price. "Um, Stephanie, did you know there's this tiny…"

"Daddy said he had to move you out of that room for maintenance. I'm sorry about that. This Lodge is quite old. There's always stuff that needs fixing."

"Well, it was more like…"

"Where are you staying now? You and your husband Jason? Is that right? I saw you skiing with him today. He seemed to be having a good time. He is quite handsome. Is that why you married him?"

"Kinda, I guess." Darla inhaled. She was trying hard not to think about the big dark emptiness overhead. "I went through this bad patch after my mom died. I was kind of pulling out of it when I got to Bennington. Jason came up to me at a party and said I was so beautiful he was going to buy me two beers. I know it sounds stupid, but it was, like, the nicest thing anyone had ever said to me. I just went head over heels. He did too, fortunately. We stayed together all through school and got married after I graduated."

"Was yours a common-law marriage?"

"Huh? Oh, yeah, I mean, no. We got married officially. Why? You got your eyes on someone? You must have your pick of the guys around here."

Stephanie drained her water glass and put it down. Looking straight at Darla she said "Alejandro", barely raising her voice above conversational level. Before Darla could figure out what in the world she meant, Alejandro himself appeared out of the gloom wearing a rumpled waiter's jacket.

"Yes mees?"

"I'd like some more water please. Darla does too."

"Yes mees."

"And I think we'll both have the Sunny Burger. That okay, Darla?"

Darla had been flipping through the dining room's thick menu and was really hoping for some grilled fish and a big salad but something in Stephanie's voice told her she had no choice. She looked up again: the spider's legs were moving now, like it was tickling itself in mid air. "Hmm, yeah, I guess."

"That's all. Lots of salt on the fries, okay Alejandro?"

"Yes mees," he said. He backed away from the table and disappeared into the dark.

Darla swallowed. How was she going to have any sort of normal conversation, much less get around to talking about selling the Lodge? She wished she was eating clam pizza with her sorority sisters back in Vermont. "Now *he's* cute," Darla said, trying the just-us-girls angle. "Is he from Mexico or something?"

"Alejandro? He's from Chile. We get a few every year. There's a special visa program where they can work here legally for the season. Daddy says that they're so grateful to be in the United States that they practically work for free. They live in the employee bunkhouse at the Ski Center so it doesn't cost us anything. And yes, he's quite handsome."

Darla picked a tortilla chip from the dented bowl in the middle of the table and bit into it. It was stale, almost rubbery. "You doin' him?"

"What?"

"Sorry. That's frat-talk. I spent so much time with Jason and his buddies when we were at Bennington that I can turn into a lout pretty much any time. What I meant was, are you sleeping with him?"

Stephanie smiled, or rather the corners of her mouth moved apart. "No," she said simply.

Darla spit the remainder of the tortilla chip into her napkin, trying to be discreet. "What about that guy on the night desk? I saw him only for a few seconds the other night, but he looked like a *fox*."

"What guy on the night desk? Carlie Mulhoney is our night clerk. She has been there since I was a little girl. Carlie lives down in Pine Butte. She works at the Big Top down there during the day and then takes our desk at night."

"Really? I swear it was a guy at the desk the other night. Totally tall dark and handsome, like a young Clint Eastwood. Maybe she found herself a boyfriend to help pass the time."

"Carlie? She is fifty years old and shaped like a doughnut. Plus I happen to know she's one of those lesbian people. That means she doesn't like men."

"Hmm. In that case it definitely wasn't her that I saw. I've actually been hoping I'd run into that guy again. He really was something."

"I'm sure it's just a misunderstanding." Stephanie folded her hands on the table in front of her and interlaced her fingers. "What's it like being married?" she said.

"Huh? Well I hardly know myself. Jason and I only got hitched two months ago." She took a deep breath. This was kind of going in a good direction. "But yeah marriage, totally takes some getting used to. I don't know if I'm ever going to get used to some guy trimming his nose hairs while I'm brushing my teeth."

Stephanie laughed, a harsh burst that she squelched by clapping her hands over her mouth. Darla smiled. It was the first time she'd seen Stephanie really react to anything. "And, I mean, how often do guys have to scratch their balls? Oh my god." Stephanie shrieked, put her hands over her face and then on the table. She seemed to be laughing but no sound was coming out. Darla wondered if she was actually choking on something. Finally Stephanie inhaled and shrieked again, her face bright red. She wiped tears from her eyes. "That sounds gross," she said.

"Oh, it's just guys. I mean, you know. Your first steady guy was probably sort of a rude surprise."

Stephanie folded her hands on the table and looked Darla in the eye. "Yes, he was," she said. She was back in control of herself once again. "Now that you mention it." She said nothing else. From the far end of the dining hall came a clatter of pots and pans, but no human voices.

Out of the dark a cold breeze blew on Darla's neck. She turned, but just missed seeing whoever it was that put the two plates of burgers and fries on the table. Stephanie was still staring straight ahead, ignoring her burger. Darla was so hungry that she wondered if she should order another burger now to save time. "Marriage is nice," she said, trying to fill the silence. "You know, it's corny but the whole thing about being with someone forever is sweet. When Jason proposed I just got *so* gushy in spite of myself."

"Oh, I know," Stephanie said. Her eyes were motionless, hard glass. "I'm engaged too."

"Really? Oh, congratulations! I didn't know. That's so exciting. Who's the lucky fella? Someone on the mountain here?"

Stephanie used her frost-colored fingernails to pick a sesame seed off her hamburger bun. She didn't touch anything else on her plate. "No, he doesn't live here anymore. But he might come back."

"No? Where does he live? Tahoe?"

Stephanie touched the sesame seed to her lips and grimaced. "Alejandro," she said, again barely raising her voice. The young man quickly appeared beside the table. "Yes mees?"

"You can take this away. It smells like some old goat."

"Yes mees. Will there be…"

"How about you Darla? Are you still working on that?"

Darla looked down at her own untouched burger. Her stomach growled but she couldn't imagine eating it. She shook her head. Alejandro took both plates and disappeared.

"He's dead," Stephanie said suddenly, her palms back on the table top. "He doesn't live anywhere because he's dead."

"Who is?"

"My fiance. He was killed in an avalanche four years ago. The same one where my brother Thad broke his back. But Andy was killed."

Darla put her hand to her mouth. "Oh I'm so sorry. I misunderstood you before. I thought you said he might be coming back to Sunny Valley. How terrible for you. You must have been devastated."

Stephanie said nothing but continued her steady gaze just over Darla's shoulder. Darla finally succumbed to the urge to turn around and look behind her but of course no one was there, just a row of empty dining tables--all set with table cloths, cutlery and wineglasses—fading into the dark. She looked back again. Stephanie was looking at her fingernails. Darla suddenly remembered the spider. She looked up but there was nothing overhead, no wiggling little bright dot in the gloom. Either it had dropped into Stephanie's hair or it was climbing back up its own endless silk rope into the blackness. Either prospect was disturbing. "Did you have to cancel your plans and everything? Return presents and stuff? I know it sounds shallow, but I would think having to deal with all that would be so…"

"No. There wasn't anything to cancel. Andy and I were going to elope. It was going to be a common-law marriage. Daddy didn't approve of our match."

"Your dad? Mr. Price? Why ever not? I mean, if two people are happy together, I think parents should just butt out."

"Daddy is possessive. I'm his baby girl, you know. And he was concerned about the business. He wants to leave it in capable hands."

Darla took a sip of water, hoping it would stop her stomach from growling. "Hmmm? What business?"

Stephanie's voice turned hard. "The Lodge, of course. And all our property in Sunny Valley. The Valley has been in my family since the Gold Rush. My grandmother left it to my mother. She left it to me. People have tried to take it away, but they can't. It's a considerable enterprise."

Darla swallowed hard. "Of course it is. I just didn't know if you had invested your, uh, profits anywhere else."

"No. Daddy built the Lodge when he got back from Vietnam. Mr. Tescher built the Ski Center. Daddy was a paratrooper. I think one of the reasons he didn't like Andy was that he was never in the Army."

"Do you mind if I ask what happened to Andy? You said there was an avalanche?"

"I wasn't here. I was in Colorado Springs."

"Training for the Olympics? That's amazing. Mr. Tescher mentioned that you were on the team."

"First alternate. GS and downhill. So I don't know what happened exactly except that Thad and Andy went into the backcountry, up Little Spring Ridge to ski some new powder. The avalanche caught them both. Daddy happened to be out there on a Ski-doo. He found Thad, who was still alive. They helicoptered him to Merced. He was very lucky. Thad didn't use to like backcountry so it's amazing he went at all, but he and Andy got along pretty well. They'd become pretty good friends."

"They'd *become* friends? Thad didn't like Andy either?"

"Not at first. He didn't at first and then he did. When we were growing up Andy would try to ski with Thad and Thad would do everything he could to lose him. It probably made them both better skiers."

"You were kids together? This Andy guy, your fiancé, grew up here too?"

Stephanie's face froze. "You are lying about the night desk," she said. "That there was a man at the night desk."

Darla's eyes opened wide. "Huh?"

A heartbeat later another crash of pots and dishes echoed into the room from the distant kitchen. Stephanie blotted her lips with her napkin. "Will you excuse me for a second?" she said.

"Of course," Darla said, swallowing hard.

Twenty minutes crawled by. The temperature in the room seemed to drop by ten degrees. There were no more sounds, no voices. Darla was puzzled and more than a little creeped out. Feeling chilled to her soul, she picked her way through the dark dining room to the lobby. No one was at the front desk, neither a handsome young Clint Eastwood or a middle-aged Lesbian shaped like a doughnut. "Hello?" she called, but heard only her own voice drifting up, lost in the dark rafters overhead.

CHAPTER 14

Thad clicked the blower to 5 and held his hands against the single round vent in the middle of the dashboard. There were lots of good things about his '65 Scout but heat wasn't one of them. His breath was fogging the windshield so much that he had to wipe it with an oily rag from the glove compartment. The bright yellow sign of Pine Butte's Big Top Market, on the other side of the parking lot, glowed unevenly through the ugly streaks.

Pine Butte was at 3,000 feet, which wasn't exactly flatland but it wasn't snow country either. Butte-heads (as Thad had called them since he was a boy) got excited over a six-inch accumulation in their driveway and were said to demand Federal assistance if it got over a foot. Some of the kids he'd known at Pine Butte High School had been pretty good skiers, but there was a difference between someone who lived *near* the snow and someone who lived *in* it. The other guys on the ski team were serious about skiing and probably skied almost as much as Thad did, but no matter how many runs they did, snow was something they ran on top of, that they had to shovel off their parent's driveway after school. It was something separate from themselves.

Thad wiped the windshield again and winced. Something about the lower elevations really set off the pain in his hip and back. He'd mentioned it to the doctor at Sutter Hospital in Merced when he went for his annual x-rays but the guy could only nod. Nobody down there understood, but why would they? If Thad went to China or something he wouldn't understand them either.

A hand thumped on the passenger side window. Thad turned in his seat and waved at the figure walking away. Alex Clipper, part of the old ski team, now running his dad's beer distributorship. Thad watched Alex cross the parking lot, pushing a baby buggy that seemed to be filled with a furry animal. Alex had been the number two skier on the team and had serious hots for Stephanie, so bad that he would drive all the way up to Sunny Valley some nights and stand shivering outside the Lodge calling her name. It was Andy who finally pulled Alex aside at school and told him to knock it off, that Stephanie didn't like it. Thad remembered it all perfectly—how he and Alex had been smoking cigarettes on the football field when Andy appeared out of nowhere. He hadn't said two words before Alex—who wrestled in the off season—started swinging. Andy, calm as ever, caught Alex's fist in mid air and used his own arm as a lever to force Alex to the ground. Thad didn't see exactly what happened but when Alex stood up again two fingers on his right hand were twisted sideways like pine saplings bent under the snow. Alex's hand was in a cast for six weeks after that. He missed the ski season and, in fact, Thad never saw Alex on skis again.

Sharp pains shot through Thad's leg and hip. He couldn't sit anywhere for very long without something for the pain and he hadn't brought a flask. He opened the door of the Scout and stepped out, careful not to slip on the clear ice puddled in the parking lot. He straightened painfully with one hand on the hood of the Scout to hold himself steady.

It was eight o'clock and the Big Top was closing. Folks were streaming out, pushing rusty shopping carts out to their trucks. The white plastic grocery bags floated over the grey asphalt like ghosts. Thad smiled briefly—in about twenty minutes half the microwaves in Pine Butte would be humming.

The doctors in Merced had given Thad a cane, an aluminum thing with a rubber handle that looked like something people would use in an old folks home. Thad hated it. He could actually get around pretty good up in Sunny Valley if he just walked on the snow and kept away from icy pavements. He used an old ski pole for support. Down in Pine Butte, though, all the sidewalks and parking lots and driveways got shoveled regularly, leaving an icy crust that was more frightening to Thad than any cornice or chute he'd skied in the Sierra or in Europe during his two years of exhibition skiing for Atomic. Thad tightened his grip on the Scout's rear view mirror, trying to keep his feet under him. He really had felt like a god during those seasons. He could ski anything, drink anything and the women had lined up outside his hotel room like they were waiting for a chair lift. Thad remembered—much too well—the power in his legs, how they could bring him out of the deepest turn, how they could find an edge in the nastiest, iciest crud. Now they felt like matchsticks, and broken ones at that.

The fluorescent lights in the Big Top flickered off and now the employees came out, pulling the yellow striped aprons over their heads and digging in their pockets and purses for cigarettes. Most of the employees were parked on the south side of the icy parking lot. As Thad watched one middle-aged woman split from the main group and walked toward the north parking lot, toward Thad. She was overweight, like most people her age in Pine Butte, and Thad knew that it took a serious amount of hairspray to hold her hair up like that after eight hours behind a register at the Big Top. Or ten hours behind the lonely front desk at the Sunny Valley Lodge, for that matter.

"Carlie!" Thad called to her, but Carlie Mulhoney was having trouble getting her cigarette lit and wasn't paying attention to anything else. The deep lines in her face became deeper as she dug cheap lighters out of her handbag, one after another, shaking and testing each one. A blast of icy wind crossed the parking lot and Carlie pulled her orange ski jacket tightly around herself. Thad had given her that jacket after his first tour.

He wondered for a moment what in the world he was doing here. So Stephanie'd heard some story that Carlie got someone else to take her shift? Well why couldn't Stephanie come all they way down here into this ice and asphalt hell and talk to Carlie herself? In fact Stephanie had seemed barely concerned—she mentioned it only in passing after her dinner with that Darla chick.

But the idea that someone unknown was behind that desk all night made Thad was uneasy, a feeling that had been popping up a lot lately. That Collins guy had said something this morning that made Thad's fingers tingle like they were being jabbed with pins. But what was it? The guy was a typical full-of-hot-air flatlander. Thad had barely paid him any attention just on principal. But something about Wallace Collins had scratched at Thad's heart, had woken him up from another dull afternoon as surely as a pair of hands around his neck.

"Carlie! Come here, get a light." She looked up finally. Carlie had been so lost in her own world that she hadn't even noticed Thad's jacked-up Scout parked next to her old Tercel. When she saw him her mouth opened wide with surprise, so wide that her unlit cigarette fell out onto the parking lot ice. She stopped in her tracks and then began to back away.

"Carlie! Carlie no, it's okay," Thad said. "I just want to talk for a minute. It's really okay." Thad tried to sound reassuring, so she wouldn't think she was in trouble, but it wasn't working. Carlie took two more frightened steps backwards and then turned, maybe to run away.

"Carlie, goddammit!" Thad could hear his father's voice inside his own, but he couldn't help it. "Get the hell over here." Thad took two steps towards Carlie but it was too many. His weak ankles twisted and suddenly both legs gave way beneath him. One hand slapped the hood of the Scout but it didn't help. Thad landed on his knees on the black ice and then collapsed completely, blind with the pain of the hard surface against his thin bones.

There was a rustling noise beside his head, white shopping bags set down in a hurry. Then Carlie was there, helping him up. "What are you thinking about?" she said. A balled up Kleenex, pulled from the depths of her ski jacket, wiped off Thad's tears of pain. "You're going to kill yourself down here."

Thad kept one arm around her shoulders, eyes and mouth shut tight, waiting for the blades of pain around his knees to subside. There had been many, many nights at the Lodge when Carlie had walked him up and down the carpet in the main hall, nights when the pain was too much for Thad to sleep, when the very thought of his own dying, withering body was too much to bear.

"Get me into the truck, Carlie," Thad said. With her help he got back in the driver's seat. He flexed his ankles—making sure there was enough feeling to drive back up the mountain. "You get in too," he said.

"Thad, now, I gotta get on home."

"Get in here." Again, his father's voice.

Thad watched silently as Carlie gathered up her groceries, locked them in her car (she had to slam the passenger door several times to get it to latch) and then climb reluctantly into the passenger's side of the Scout. Thad had already pressed the dashboard cigarette lighter so it was ready for her when she got in. Carlie lit her cigarette, took a deep draft off it, rolled the window down two inches and blew the smoke out into the icy parking lot.

Thad waited, gave her time to smoke. After two more puffs she wiped her eyes with the sleeves of her jacket. "I didn't see no harm in it," she said finally. Black stuff smeared off onto the orange sleeves, which Thad realized after a moment was eye makeup and not motor oil. "Nights up there are dead quiet any more. All I do is watch the Price Club and go to sleep." She sniffed and dug into the deep jacket pockets for more wadded-up Kleenex. "Your family's been real good to me. Stephanie, you, your dad, your ma…"

Thad ran his hands through his hair. So it was true. There was some-one. "It's okay, Carlie. Stop crying, okay? Someone else has been taking your shift at the Lodge? Why didn't you just tell us? You got yourself an-other night job down here? Or a new boyfriend?"

Carlie didn't laugh. Thad searched her face, which was smeared with tears and black eye makeup. She shook her head slowly from side to side, her jaw quivering. "No, I don't have no other job. He's not taking the pay or nothing."

Thad reached over, took the cigarette out of her fingers and tapped off the long ash. She was so upset she'd forgotten to smoke. Thad smoked the last inch and flicked the butt out the window. The parking lot outside was completely deserted, the harsh yellow lights showing only crushed coffee cups and dirty piles of snow shoved into the corners by contract plows. The emptiness sank into Thad. He knew the next question would only make it worse. "Who's taking your shift?" he said. "Who the hell would want to sit in that stinking old lodge all night for free? C'mon Carlie. You can tell me."

Carlie was paralyzed. Her face was frozen hard, her jaw clamped shut. The only sign she was still alive was the steady stream of black tears dripping onto the orange sleeves of her jacket. Thad had never seen her so upset, never imagined it. She inhaled, a desperate gulp, and then clawed at her face with her long red fingernails. "I thought he was a ghost. I god-honest did. I don't believe in nothing like that, but, but I god-honest thought he was a ghost. He ain't no ghost, though. He killed Pringles."

"Your cat? Who did? Who killed Pringles?"

"I don't know why. I would have kept quiet, I swear I woulda. But he killed her anyway."

Thad's legs, which he could barely feel at the best of times, went completely numb. The dread that had hovered on the edge of his consciousness now grew to a full revelation. "Is he back?" Thad's voice was a hoarse, constricted whisper. "Are you saying he's back?"

Carlie had wrapped herself completely in Thad's old ski jacket. A few stiff curls of hair poked out the top. They nodded. Thad felt his fingers turn numb too. "He's alive and he's been walking around the Lodge in the middle of the night?" Thad said, incredulous. "While we're all asleep?"

Again, the curls nodded.

CHAPTER 15

When Stephanie said it was my seventeenth birthday. I believed her. No one had ever mentioned my birthday in the years I had lived in Sunny Valley, but I would believe anything she told me.

"C'mon." She came into my basement room late at night while I was sleeping, dreaming of her. She watched, happy but impatient, while I pulled on my wool sweater and old ski jacket and pants. We crept out the back door of the Lodge into the still and bitter night. It was so cold that the inside of my nostrils stuck together. I barely noticed. She ran laughing through the empty snow field beside the Lodge while I chased. I couldn't keep up, of course. Stephanie was a miracle on ice or snow, a silver light that never faded.

She stopped at the front door of Lance Stewart's ski shop. I slid the last few icy feet and we crashed together onto the bank of snow shoveled up beside the front door. I unzipped her down jacket and put one hand on the tight silk thermal shirt that covered her stomach. The air temperature was well below zero but her skin burned. I pressed myself down on top of her and found her lips. They were hot too, searing me forever. I walked my fingertips over silk and touched her breast lightly with my nails. Stephanie pushed me off. "Not now, doofus," she said. She zipped herself back into her quilted jacket. "We got stuff to do."

She pulled a big ring of keys from her jacket pocket and gave them to me. Then she pointed at Lance's front door. "Open it," she said.

I was no different from anyone else in Sunny Valley in that I could never question her, never refuse her. I tried the keys in succession until I found the right ones for the door and the deadbolt. In a few seconds we were inside the shop, standing between mannequins in expensive ski parkas. She switched on the lights, unafraid. "Gosh those are ugly," she said. "Flatlander ugly."

We walked back to the rental shop where Stephanie quickly picked through the racks and took down a pair of skis. "These're practically new," she said, "and they've got bindings mounted already. What's your boot size?" I had no idea. The boots I skied in were Thad's castoffs. With steady seriousness, Stephanie sat me down in Lance's boot department and measured my feet with a little machine. I closed my eyes and melted back into the chair as she held each foot in her hands, feeling the heel, the arch, the toes. "Wake up," she said finally. "You're an eleven. Go outside and make sure the coast is clear."

I went back out into the stiff cold, waiting while Stephanie bumped and crashed inside. Of course the coast was clear. The highway froze solid at night. The sand truck made its last trip at midnight, putting just enough grip on the ice so that Nate Tescher--who went down to drink in the bars in Pine Butte almost every night—would have a hope of getting home alive.

"Let's go." Stephanie came outside, lugging brand new ski and boot bags, both full.

I stopped at the door. "Stephanie, that's expensive stuff."

"Don't be stupid. It's your birthday. You don't have to pay."

"I don't?"

"No, doofus. Lance told me it was okay."

I let her convince me, though I knew it wasn't true. I barely knew Lance. The last time I'd seen him was a month earlier when Bucky sent me to the shop to buy a pair of gloves for a guest at the Lodge. Lance, squinting through cigarette smoke, rang up the sale and then let the gloves fall to the floor for me to pick up.

If you weren't ski patrol, one of his Flying Coyotes, you didn't exist for Lance. I was as good a skier as most of them but I hadn't been invited to join. I was still a flatlander in their eyes, though I'd been in the valley for seven years. And there were things about the Coyotes I didn't understand. "Coyotes got this ritual," Thad had told me. "You've got to kill something. They make you bring something important to you and you kill it."

"Why?" I had said. "What did you kill?"

Thad shrugged. "Some dog. You just gotta prove the Coyotes come first."

We were stacking firewood outside in the bright afternoon sun, but the sweat froze on my neck. It was Thunder he was talking about. Thunder the ancient black Labrador that had belonged to Stephanie's mother. Thunder did very little anymore besides doze on the broad granite slab that made up the hearth of the Lodge's great fireplace. Stephanie's grandparents were buried under that stone, I knew, and it seemed that Thunder, in his old age, had appointed himself guardian of their tomb. The dog disappeared a few years ago and everyone assumed it had wandered off into the snow to die on its own. Now I knew the truth. Now I knew the real price of joining Lance's Coyotes. What did I have that meant so much, that I could sacrifice? Nothing. I had nothing. They would never let me join because I had nothing to give.

I locked the door to the shop and gave Stephanie back the keys. We walked towards the Lodge down the middle of the street under a nearly full moon, carrying probably a thousand dollars worth of stolen ski equipment. A few days ago I'd spent half an hour hanging from Bucky's pullup bar because I'd used a torn kitchen towel to dewax my old skis, but tonight I was fearless, laughing inside and out. I was with Stephanie and this was Sunny Valley, the place where law, physics and human nature all adapted to suit her.

We walked a short way into the woods behind the Lodge, kicking into the snow's icy crust. We dropped the ski bags behind a big fir and tried to hide them in the snow but the crust was frozen too hard for us to do more than spread a few crystals. No matter. Stephanie declared them to be invisible so that was enough.

We stepped back out of the trees into the clearing behind the hulking blackness of the Lodge. The moon had set and stars ignited the sky. She faced me and now she opened my jacket, eagerly pulling the Velcro patches apart (the zipper had never worked). She put her hands inside, feeling my chest and stomach through my shirt. We'd been outside in paralyzing cold for nearly an hour but still her hands burned on me, just as her breath seared my neck, my chin, my lips. Her fingers found a hole in my shirt near the shoulder. She worried it, spread it and then pulled, ripping me open to the night. She sucked at my collarbone and then on my right nipple, stone hard from the cold but now plunged into fire. I felt teeth. I put my hands in her hair and gripped hard.

Then she pulled away and there was only the cold air on my wet and open chest. Already she had pulled on her hat and mittens.

"Meet me here tomorrow morning. At eight." She was all business now, as if planning a class picnic. "I'm going to teach you something new."

And then she was gone, moving lightly over the snow crust, leaving me standing, without breath, slowly turning to ice under the blazing stars.

CHAPTER 16

Thad felt the rear wheels of the Scout start to slip. He pulled at the loose denim around his knee to ease his foot off the gas. With his left hand he nudged the steering wheel to the right, in the opposite direction of the turn. The county kept Highway 6 pretty well plowed, but the road had its own treachery. During the day Sierra sunshine melted the roadside snowbanks so that sheets of water flowed across the road. The wet corners were slippery enough during the day, but after the sun went down they froze into ice slicks, perfectly placed to catch a flatlander SUV and throw it spinning into the snow bank. Roger Wilkins drove the county sand truck up and down the highway until about midnight on most evenings, but you still had to be careful.

Thad had been driving Highway 6 since he was twelve years old and before his injury he'd given no more thought to the ice curves than he gave to the fat-assed skiers he had to slalom around on Sunny Valley's blue runs. Now though, with his legs barely able to push the Scout's pedals, he really had to pay attention.

Thad wiggled a knob on the dash until the windshield wipers came on. They made three passes over the glass, sweeping away most of the snow, and then stopped. It was starting to snow heavily now that he was above the six thousand foot mark. At this rate there would be a good three feet of fresh snow on the mountain by morning. By noon Stephanie would have carved it all up with her distinctive long turns.

Sharp pain arced from Thad's hip to his knee, temporarily waking the nerves to the point where he could actually wiggle his toes. He pushed the accelerator harder. Stephanie was up at the Lodge and that madman was up there too, if Carlie was right. If she wasn't the one totally off her rocker. If it *was* him, why hadn't he done anything yet? He'd been on Carlie's shift for nearly a week. He could have done anything he wanted to any of them by now. Anything. The fact that he hadn't was the best argument that, whoever it was that had bullied his way into the Lodge, it wasn't Andy. But Thad wasn't convinced.

He wiggled the switch and then smashed a fist against the glass. The wipers woke up again, moving sluggishly from side to side. Not that Thad needed them. He could drive Highway 6 in a thick storm without wipers if he had to. He'd actually done it once just to prove it, with a terrified Alex Clipper in the passenger seat.

The forecast was for cold dry snow, lots of it, over the next day and into the weekend. The skies had been sunny and clear for most of the previous week, so four feet of fresh new snow on top of a slick, compressed layer of old snow meant the worst avalanche conditions. The Coyotes would be out early tomorrow dropping explosive charges into the big cornices at the boundaries of the ski area, shaking loose the deadly hanging snow masses. They wouldn't work Little Spring Ridge, of course. No one went up there any more.

Thad exhaled deeply and watched his breath fill the cab. Pain gnawed at his legs and lower back. There'd been a dump like this the night before the accident. Stephanie had seen the grey cloud over California on a TV weatherman's map and called Thad from the Olympic training camp in Colorado Springs.

"I can't believe you've got powder, you dog," she said. "All we're doing here is lifting weights and running around a track. I thought the ski team was supposed to ski."

Thad remembered the blinding hangover he'd had that night, so bad that even moving his lips was painful. "I can't talk to you right now, doll," he'd said, wincing "Dad's got some stuff for me to do."

"What stuff? Since when do you do anything Daddy says?"

It was too much. Way too much. "I just can't talk right now. Do you want me to get Andy?"

"Who?" There was laughter on the other end, light as snow flakes blown off the end of ski tips. "Is *he* still working there?"

"Stephanie don't talk like that."

"Tell mister mopey to stop sending me his bad poetry. If he does I'll send him an autographed tee shirt from the United States Olympic Training Camp in Colorado Springs, Colorado."

Thad's windpipe had constricted so much he could barely breathe. "Don't say that," he'd whispered, but Stephanie had already hung up.

Grady Flat went past. Only eight miles to go, though they were the coldest and windiest of the whole stretch between Pine Butte and Sunny Valley. Goddamn Stephanie anyway. She was probably lying in the middle of the big hall right now with her neck broken. What did Thad care?

He let up the gas, slowing in anticipation of an upcoming sharp bend to the left. It was the site of a lot of fender benders in the summer because the far side of the turn overlooked the deep granite of Stanislaus Valley, a spectacular view falling steeply away from Highway 6. Flatlanders would invariably slow down in the middle of the turn to gawk at the view, only to be slammed from behind by a local late for work.

The back of the Scout slid again but Thad was ready. He pressed the wheel against the turn and felt the Scout straighten. Had Andy really come back? Why? What was he planning to do to Bucky, or Stephanie, or Thad himself, for that matter? What punishment could possibly fit their collective crimes?

With so much snow flying it was hard to judge the bend exactly. Thad leaned forward and wiped the windshield with his hand, squinting into the white blur ahead. A motion caught his eye, something falling off the high side of the bend. A small avalanche? It was dark, a dark blue shape. A coyote?

A skier.

The barely visible shape landed square in the middle of Thad's lane. Thad jerked the steering wheel instinctively, oversteering. It was impossible to do anything else. The rear of the Scout slid forward until the whole truck was sliding sideways, heading for the guardrail. It was an effortless skid for a few feet until the wheels left the icy pavement and hit the gravel on the shoulder. The wheels stopped and the momentum of the top-heavy Scout caused it to roll like a bowling ball, tipping over the guardrail and plunging into the granite valley below.

Funny. After all the surgery and physical therapy Thad had taken down in Modesto, he could feel his legs and lower torso better now than ever before—now that he'd been thrown through the windshield of the wrecked, tumbling Scout and into an icy hole at the base of a big Douglas Fir. Thad could move nothing, but every single nerve below his waist was more awake now than anytime since the avalanche, crying out with four years worth of stored pain. It wouldn't last, though. His toes and fingertips were turning numb, the newly awakened nerves dying by inches. Now his heel, now his ankles. Soon his knees and thighs would be dead, his cock, his abs, his lungs. In some ways he was grateful that the endless deterioration of his old spinal injury, his slow self consumption, was finally at an end.

There was a swishing sound nearby, skis running expertly through the trees. Thad smiled. He heard the click of bindings and the sound of skis being thrust into the snow. A gloved hand cleared his face. Thad's scalp was numb. He tried to inhale but could only make a tiny breath. His lungs seemed to be filled with packed snow.

"You had your chence." The voice seemed to come from all around, swirling in the falling snow. "I gev you a fair shot. You could have run me over. You were weak."

Thad smiled and nodded. It was just like Andy. Fair and honest to a fault. Fair unto death. Thad braced himself, dug his fingernails into his palms against the barbs of pain that were to come. He inhaled as deeply as he could and felt the tears squeeze out his eyes. His neck was dying, his jaw, his lips. He had only one chance.

"It was a mistake," Thad said. The pain tried to close his throat but Thad dug into his palms hard. "She made that deal with Dad and Tescher but she never signed the papers. She was going to come back to you after the Olympics. The two of you would have owned Sunny Valley. She loved you." Thad's face was hard now, a stiff mask wrapped in fire. He pushed his lips together with his last strength. "She still loves you."

Andy stood up and pulled a pair of climbing skins from his pack. Thad watched with paralyzed eyes as Andy strapped them onto his skis for the climb back up to Highway 6.

"Two feet due tonight," he said. "That'll hide you until spring. I'll come back then and bury you before the coyotes find you. I owe you thet."

With one eye closed, Thad saw Andy strap on his poles and kick into his bindings. He turned and started up the hill. The skins on the bottom of his skis gripped the snow.

Thad's eyes both closed. Their sockets filled with falling snow.

CHAPTER 17

It seems like ancient history to me, a tale I might have read in a dusty history book, but there was a time when Sunny Valley's ski slopes were crowded, full of weekenders in their bright ski jackets, their children falling and crying on the bunny hill.

The Lodge was bright and full of life, with stacks of luggage in the hallways and skis lining the racks outside. It was so busy, in fact, that during my first years in Sunny Valley I didn't have to work on Saturdays. Bucky actually hired two cleaners for the weekends and it was only on weekdays and Sundays, that I had to help.

Saturdays were my own. On Saturday I could ski from the moment the lifts creaked to life in the morning, when the runs were still rock hard with ice, until the very end of the day, when I would wait at the top of the mountain and watch the flatlanders and their squalling children climb into their cars, wet and exhausted. They had to leave but I could take one more run, with legs burning, lungs scraping from the icy late afternoon air, one more run, the best of the day.

On the Saturday after Stephanie stole my new skis from Lance's shop, we didn't go to Tescher's mountain to ski. Instead we met in the wooded slope behind the Lodge. She helped me get into the bindings, which were different from what I was used to.

"They're broken," I said, wiggling my boot. The toe was securely clamped in the binding but the heel swung free.

She laughed, her you-don't-know-anything laugh. "They're supposed to be that way, doofus. That way we can climb Little Spring ridge and ski some stuff that no one else has touched."

"Climb the ridge?" I said.

Stephanie pushed, catching me off balance. I toppled over sideways onto the snow. She grabbed each of my skis and pulled a yellow cloth over the bases. "These are skins," she said. "People used to use real seal skins. Skins grab the snow so you can climb."

She reached a hand down to help me up. I tried to pull her on top of me but she was ready for that old trick and slipped out of her silver mitten. I held a handful of air.

"Quit fooling around," she said. She was oddly abrupt that morning, like a school teacher. "Let's go."

Stephanie was moving up into the trees before I was even back on my feet. I put my skis in her tracks and followed behind. The skins really did grip the snow, so you could essentially ski uphill. Eventually, though, we would have to ski back down and I wondered about the free-heel binding, how I would get the lift-and-turn motion I had learned from Stephanie and Tescher and Thad.

She was climbing nearly straight up and my lungs burned trying to catch her. At first she was only a white and silver flash up ahead, but after half an hour of really pushing, I caught up to the point where I could see her pale hair pulled back tight into a pony tail. The sun was well up now and I was perspiring, soaking in my old sweater and jeans. I kicked my skis in to get a good grip on the slope. Stephanie, as usual, moved effortlessly over the snow, barely making an indentation. I couldn't hear her breath over my own rasping.

She stopped at the treeline and waited for me to catch up. We were just below some volcanic bluffs that I knew very well. They were visible from the north-facing rooms of the Lodge and on my cleaning days I would sometimes explore the bluffs in my mind. Someone had told me that coyote and cougar lived in the caves under the bluffs and I imagined myself living with them, sharing their kill.

"There's two routes here," Stephanie said, pointing toward the ridge with her ski pole. "You can either go to the right of the bluffs, which is faster, or you can go here on the left side. The left side is easier but there's actually a little chute at the very top where you have to take your skis off and kick with your boots the rest of the way up."

"But where are we going?" I said. "It's *Saturday*." I wondered if maybe this was some back way to the top of the ski area, but we were heading in exactly the wrong direction. And if we climbed all the way to the bluff top I wasn't sure I'd have much leg left for a full day's skiing.

"Shut up," she said. "If you want to go and ski with a bunch of flat-landers and snowboarders, go ahead. Go ahead and go back down right now."

"No."

"Then shut up and listen. I showed you the two routes. One thing to remember is that the far one gets a lot of wind drift after a storm. The cornices can be really unstable. Look down here. See it?"

"See what?"

"The avalanche chute. See that section of ridge below the bluffs? See how it's all scoured out? Where there's no trees for a few hundred yards? That's the chute. There's a good-sized avalanche there almost every year. It's not a safe area, but all you need to do is wait a few days for the snow to consolidate and then you're okay. Do you understand?"

"Sure."

"I'm serious. We *should* be wearing avalanche beacons. You should always wear one up here. Promise me."

"I don't have an avalanche beacon."

"I know that. I'll get you one. Until then just promise me you'll only come up here when it's safe."

"I'll only come up with you."

"That's not true. Just promise me, okay?"

"Okay."

"Let's go then." She chose the western route, a long gradual slog under the bluffs. The sun was full on the open ridge face now. Stephanie took off her ski jacket and tied it around her waist. When we got to the chute I helped her climb over. I put my hands on her, feeling her strong legs through her ski pants. Her skin was hot. It always was.

From the top we could see all of Sunny Valley – the Lodge, the village, the parking lot and lifts of the ski area. The parking lot was full and I could see black specks all over the groomed blue runs on the south side of the mountain. It seemed downright strange not be over there on a Saturday, but here I was on the top of the wrong ridge, wearing some weird skis, exhausted from the climb. I was with Stephanie thought, so in one very important sense the core of my being was complete, but I still didn't see how we were going to get any skiing done on my one day of freedom.

She showed me how to take the climbing skins off of my skis and stow them in my pack. "Ready?" she said.

"Hmm? For what?"

"When did it snow last?"

"About a week ago."

"Is there any powder left on Mr. Tescher's mountain? If we went skiing up there today, you think we'd find any?"

I laughed. Stephanie herself was the worst powder pig of them all. After a dump she would ski all day until the last pocket of soft weightless snow was tracked and destroyed. More than once she had made them keep the lifts open for an hour or so past closing so that she could ski the last hidden powder in the canyon and in the trees.

"What would you give to do a powder run right now?" she said. "Totally untracked. What would you do?"

"Anything."

"Would you kiss me?"

She could be coy. She could tease. She could think one thing, *feel* one thing, and say another. I never could. I wanted to play the game too, to do something to show her I wasn't just a mindless slave, but I couldn't. I reached down and put my hand on the side of her face, my fingers under the base of her skull. My thumb found her mouth, explored it, and then rubbed her saliva over her lips.

I pulled her close. We kissed and I felt the same unholy burn pulse through me that I felt every time she was near. I felt weak—I wanted to fall, to put my face into her warm skin.

"Don't," she said. "We got stuff to do."

"What stuff?"

She cracked me in the ear with her elbow. "C'mon."

We pushed across the ridge top to the opposite edge. It was the top of a huge north-facing bowl that I had never seen before, that I had never even dreamed of. Beyond it was an incredible vista of Sierra granite and snow.

"Let's pay attention this time," Stephanie said. It was something Te-scher always said to the race team. "You've got good balance, Andy," she said, "but these are Telemark skis. There's some extra stuff you have to remember."

"I've forgotten everything already," I said.

She didn't laugh but instead put on her school teacher face. There was no point in trying to distract her. Stephanie had spent hundreds of hours teaching me to ski over the years. It was the one thing she really cared about.

She tucked herself into a crouch, and split her legs, one forward and back. "Bend your front knee a little but stay centered over the skis. The weird thing is that you want to keep your weight *back*. It's totally different from alpine. Drop your knee, start your turn with the rear ski, feel it catch, and then lift and drop the other knee."

Without another word Stephanie launched over the lip into the north bowl. The face was steep but wide open and from her first line I could see that the snow was as dry and fluffy as if it had fallen that morning. I was amazed: it had been a week since the last storm but here the snow was perfect, trackless powder. It was as if she had created it, conjured it up just for us.

Stephanie liked long carving lines but on this run she made tight, symmetric esses, showing me the free heel technique. Her turns were beautiful and she was even more fluid, more dynamic than she was on conventional skis. Stephanie in motion was a revelation, but to see her weightless in the snow, not locked into her skis but floating with them, was an image of silver beauty right out of our poetry book. The words I had been struggling to write she now made true.

I followed, trying to mimic her technique. I took a spectacular fall af-ter only four turns, but I felt it. The silver poetry was in me now too. It might take years for me to master this new technique, these Telemark skis, but I knew it was where I wanted to go. I wouldn't be spending my Saturdays dodging the sluggish skiers at the mountain anymore. I got up and shook the lovely powder snow off my jacket. Taking a deep breath I dropped into the bowl again, moving my legs like I was walking on air.

We climbed back up and took another run through a fresh powder line, this time with Stephanie behind me yelling instructions. "Get your fat butt *back*. You're skiing like a flatlander." I tried. My mind knew what I wanted to do—my heart knew it—but it would be a little while until the rest of me could figure it out.

It was noon when we climbed out of the bowl. Stephanie took us through some trees a little west of our earlier runs to show me another, steeper chute. She pushed ahead and I struggled to keep up. At the top of the ridge I found her bending over some tracks in the snow. She had taken off her skis. As I watched she let a drop of spit fall between her lips.

"Daddy was up here," she said. "These are his tracks. You can get a Ski-doo up here but you have to start all the way back on Highway 6."

"Why would your dad come up here?"

She took a deep breath. "Mama's buried up here, for one. Did you know that?" Stephanie looked south, along the ridge. "Way out there on the point. He used to come up here all the time when he was young. He told us all about it. He was the only Telemark skier in Sunny Valley for a long time. He taught me. He taught Thad but Thad's too lazy to come all the way up here." She took a deep breath and looked down at the Lodge. "I never see his tracks up here anymore though. It's been years and years."

For a moment Stephanie looked small, a little girl lost the snow. "Do you know anything about poison?" she said. "Arsenic and stuff?"

I put my hand up through her jacket, untucked her thermal shirt and put my fingertips into the hollow of her back. There was a tiny nest of golden hairs there, I knew, and I found them with my fingertips. Stephanie took a small breath and then reached up and caught my earlobe in her teeth. A sharp pain pierced through to my groin.

"Do you how to kill Andy?" she said into my ear. Her hot breath melted me. Her tongue touched the edges of my ear and now she was reaching down, unbuttoning my jeans. "Will you *help* me?"

I hardly heard her. I pulled the long zipper on the side of her snow pants. She whipped them off, lay them on the snow and pushed me down on top of them. Before I could recover my breath from the cold sting of snow on my skin she was on top of me, putting me inside her. She grabbed my shoulders with her fists and dug her fingernails deep. That heat that was always part of Stephanie surrounded me now and even though I was lying on my back in the snow, sweat covered my stomach and chest. She leaned her head over and let her hair drop across my face, blinding me. She ground her body into mine, carving me the way she did a powdery hillside.

"You *jerk*," she said between breaths. "You stupid, stupid *jerk*." Her nails dug deeper and I was lost into her, a hopeless moment of blood, ice, and desperate, endless pleasure. I relived every sensation of my entire life. Pain, fear and hunger. Tears and loneliness. The burn of endless asphault streets and the cold of Bucky Price's chin-up bar. The sharp knife of wind on top of the mountain before the last run of the day. The nameless pleasure of watching her, Stephanie, float through the pines like a silver bird. The nights alone in the dark of the Lodge, wanting only one thing in the world, the one thing in the world that was now mine, entirely mine.

A shadow crept across my shoulder. It wasn't the glare of the Sierra sun that woke us up but the deep chill of its shadows. Stephanie shivered and pulled my sweater closer around her neck. I tried to cover her with my hands, but she raised herself up, her elbows digging into my chest.

"You're *cold*," she said.

"I've been lying on the snow for an hour."

"Get up then."

She stood up and pulled her clothes on, stopping only to throw snow on me as I tried to pull on my jeans. My muscles had turned to stone and I felt strangely disoriented.

"You won't forget what you promised me?"

I untangled my blue sweater, which was sopping wet. I didn't want to answer but she came close again and kissed me. "Do you remember?"

"You want me to kill someone" I said. "Who?"

"You know who. I don't have to tell you."

I wrapped my arms around myself, trying to find warmth. "I'll kill him," I said. "I won't use rat poison either."

"You should use poison, Andy. You know he was in the Army."

"You have to tell me why, though." I wasn't sure if I was kidding or not. I wasn't sure what, if anything, of the last few hours was real.

Stephanie was on one knee setting her bindings. She seemed the same person as ever. In some ways so was I. I'd been her prisoner since the first moment I had seen her. Now I was her prisoner and more.

"So what?" I threw a little snow her way, trying to tease out her mood.

Stephanie was mostly dressed. She tightened her pack straps. She looked at the sky, the sun, and then into the south-side couloir at her feet, the top of the avalanche chute leading down into Sunny Valley.

"Just remember you promised me."

A sharp gust came up the ridge. My eyes watered. She was serious. I could see that she was ready to drop into the couloir, to do one of those huge arcing turns that only she could do, that the rest of the skiers in the valley could only watch gape-mouthed. I grabbed her by her silver collar. "Why?" I said.

"Because he's a jerk."

"You called me a jerk."

"I did not."

"You did. While we were screwing."

She wrinkled her nose. "You're not that kind of jerk."

I put my thumb behind her jaw and found the painful spot just under her ear. Thad used to do it to me all the time when we were little.

"Don't," Stephanie said.

"Just tell me. I'll kill him if you want me to. I'll do anything. But you have to tell me."

She took a deep breath and then shook herself out of my grip.

"You wouldn't understand."

"No one understands you better."

She exhaled. "Okay," she said. "Look across the valley over at the other ridge."

"At the mountain? At the Ski Center?"

"Yeah. See all those drops? Riley's Cup, Bonfire, all that. See it?"

"Yeah, of course."

"You've seen me ski there, right?"

I didn't say anything. There had never been a more ridiculous question.

"Have you ever seen anyone ski it better? I mean really. Tell me honestly. Not just because you love me or anything, but tell me the truth. Have you ever seen anyone ski it better? Thad or anyone?"

"No. Of course not."

"Thad can drop in there, but he doesn't really *ski* it, does he? He just drops in and drops out." Stephanie pulled her hands out of her pole straps and threw the poles on the snow. She stripped off her gloves and threw them down too. "So why did *he* get recommended for the Olympic tryouts year before last and I didn't? Why?"

I said nothing. There was wind, cold wind, but Stephanie was taking off her jacket. Her breasts, sculpted under silk, stood out hard in the cold. She was about to tear off her ski pants when she realized that she was still locked into her skis. "Darn! Darn!" She ripped at the buckles. "Skiers under 16 have to have a regional board member sign for them before they can go to the tryouts. Stupid Billy Edison down in Pine Butte got signed. I didn't. Why didn't I get signed?"

I stood open mouthed and confused. A terrible unease crept over me. "I don't know, Stephanie," I said.

"I know you don't, doofus. Mr. Tescher is the regional board member for this district. He's the one who's supposed to sign people on. He didn't do it last time and he's not going to sign me again next year."

"How do you know?"

"Because we own Sunny Valley, Daddy and me. Mr. Tescher thinks Daddy stole it from him when Daddy married Mr. Tescher's sister."

"Your mom was Mr. Tescher's sister? I didn't know that. But how will it help if I kill Bucky? How will that get you on the Olympic team?"

Stephanie was naked now except for her black ski boots, but not shivering, only holding me in her burning stare. "What are you doing?" she said. "Why are you standing there?"

I fumbled out of my gear. Did she really want to make love again in the shadowy cold?

"Come here. Kneel down."

I dropped to my knees in the snow. She came to me and pressed her stomach to my waiting lips, wrapping her arms around my head. She was still warm, but I could feel her fire dimming.

She leaned down and kissed my forehead and then my eyes. I was kneeling bare-legged in the snow. The raw cold shot pain into my knees and shins.

"Mr. Tescher will do what I say once Daddy is gone," Stephanie said. "But he'll never stop trying to get the Valley. I need you to protect me."

I shivered. She stroked my hair. "That's how it works in Sunny Valley. When we're married, you'll protect me and our little baby girl. Women own the valley and the men protect us. That's how it works."

She kissed my forehead again. I was shivering so hard I thought my skull would crack against her teeth. She leaned down and again bit my earlobe. This time she bit hard but I was literally frozen into place, unable to let go of her. There was a warm trickle of blood and I felt her tongue licking in and out, around and below my ear.

"We'll get married," she said. "It will be forever. Even after we die. It's no good if it's just while we're alive. We'll have a little baby, a little girl. If I'm not here, you'll protect her too. It has to be forever."

I began to cry. I felt weak, near death. It seemed like she was about to disappear, to somehow lift right into the sky. The idea that she might die, that I might someday be left alone by myself in this cruel valley, was overwhelming.

"Stay with me," I said. "Don't ever leave."

"I never will," she whispered. "That's how it works. You take care of me, protect me. Do this for me and I will be with you forever."

CHAPTER 18

Jason regarded the plywood-covered door with suspicion. A faded sign overhead said "Growler's Pizza."

"I dunno Mr. Collins," Jason said. "This place looks closed. Like it's been closed for years."

"Nonsense. I'm sure Kyle said there was someplace we could eat in the village. I hope we're not too late for lunch. I'm starving." Wallace Collins punched his skis into a snow drift near the front door. "It does look a little run down, but everything is here, Jason. It wouldn't be such a good deal otherwise." Collins exhaled loudly. "I've seen cheerier pizza parlors, that's for sure. Perhaps you might want to take this place over, Jason. It could be a fun project for you. Food service. You could even have live music."

"Sure," Jason said doubtfully. He wiggled the door latch and then put his face against the cracked window, using his gloved hand to shade out the blue glare of daylight. "I can't see anything. There's cardboard over these windows or something. And the door's locked."

Wallace Collins pushed Jason aside. "I can *hear* voices inside. Can't you ? Sounds like a child's birthday party or something. And there are fresh boot prints all over here." He rattled the door. "Those fools. Someone has locked the door in the middle of the day and they haven't even noticed. No wonder this place loses money."

"Mr. Collins…"

Collins hammered the door with his gloved fist. "These folks have a lot to learn. This is a fire hazard, you know. If the fire marshal were to hear about this they could be in for a big fine."

"I just don't think…"

Collins hammered again. "OPEN UP. You've got paying customers out here."

There was a noise like furniture being shoved aside and then a series of latches thrown. The door squeaked open barely a hand's breadth, enough for a plume of hot air to escape. With it came the stench of beer, marijuana smoke, and male sweat. Collins stepped back, blinking. The door started to close again but he threw himself forward and put his ski boot in the gap before it slammed shut. Behind the smell, a roar of voices poured out into the harsh daylight. "Open this door," Collins said. "Open it or I'll call the police."

The gap widened enough for them to see the face behind it, Alejandro, one of the Chilean lift operators. The room was dim behind him, lit by candles and a few gas lamps scattered unevenly.

"Is closed," Alejandro said.

"How can you be closed? It's lunch time. Let us in or we'll take our business elsewhere."

"Come back later."

"I'll come back later alright. We'll come back when…" Wallace Collins suddenly leaned forward. "Is that my son in there? Is that Kyle? Is that my son?" Collins shoved the door with his shoulder, knocking Alejandro backwards, but once in the room Collins stopped. "My god," he said. "What is this place?

Kyle was just inside the door, sitting on a beer keg on Collin's left. He stared straight ahead, as if in a daze. His mouth hung open in a dead circle and blood dripped down his chin and over his white thermal shirt.

"Kyle!"

Laughter erupted from every corner of the dark room, harsh squawks and catcalls. Collins could make out a dozen shapes perched on kegs and cardboard boxes, or sprawled on cushions ripped from dining chairs. The only table in the room had three legs and stood at a crazy angle in the center. Collins walked up to his son and took his chin in his hand, smearing the blood with his thumb. "My god," he said. "What has happened to you?" Kyle looked at Collins blearily at first, without any sort of recognition. His eyes finally focused. "Dad," he said. "Fuckin' Dad." Kyle let his head fall back. He laughed, a barking, idiotic cackle. Wallace Collins's hand was left in mid air, full of blood.

Another wave of laughter sliced the room and a bottle smashed somewhere behind him. The shapes in the corners were hooting now in unison like mad owls. Collins could see that many were wearing absurd Halloween masks, grey plastic images of a dog or a fox.

A huge man stood in the center of the room. His ski bib was undone at the shoulder and had slipped down to gather around his knees. His thermal underwear was pulled down too and he was holding his thick penis in one hand, urinating into a wine bottle while tilting unsteadily on his feet. The fat man wore one of the grey dog masks but it covered hardly any of his wide red face or the wet mouth behind. Collins had no trouble recognizing Nate Tescher, but Tescher evidently had not seen Collins.

"Where's our boy?" Tescher bellowed into the room, weaving from side to side. Scattered cheers and howls rose from the shadows. "Where's our new Coyote? He passed the test. Time for a baptism. He's earned it." Tescher took a wheezing breath. "I'm going to need another bottle, you assholes. Huh *huh* . Get me another bottle."

A beer bottle flew out of one corner. It missed Tescher's head and smashed at Collins's feet. Tescher flung his own bottle toward the same corner, spraying urine over half the room. Dog-masked boys dove to get out of the way. "You're dead now," Tescher said, tucking himself in. "I'm going to whup your ass back to chili or wherever it is you beaners come from. Where's our boy? Get up here!"

Tescher had his ski bib almost back up over his stomach when Collins grabbed his arm, trying to spin him around. Tescher didn't budge.

"Nate."

"Get away from me."

"*Nate.*"

Tescher turned around and slowly peeled off his dog mask. "Well I'll be damned. Wallace Collins. Huh *huh* . How the hell did you get in here? You don't own my mountain yet, and you sure as shit don't own Price's old pizza parlor. Go back to Pussyville. You're disrupting our, uh, meeting."

"What has happened to my son? He is badly injured, perhaps concussed. I insist…"

"Little Kyle? Concussed? The Coyotes would never hurt a fly. He just found the nitrous oxide bottle, that's all. Isn't that right Kylie?"

Both turned. Kyle was still sitting in the corner, dull and bloody. His face was streaked with tears.

"Poor Kylie." Groans passed around the room as Tescher picked something up off the floor and held it against Kyle's face. It took Collins a moment to realize it was some kind of gas mask and Tescher was turning the handle on a steel tank near his feet.

"Nate."

Kyle was laughing again, cackling like an animal.

"Nate, stop this nonsense. I demand…"

"See Collins? Huh *huh*. That's all it takes. It's a pity I never had children. I would have made a great father." He held the mask to his own face and took a sniff, smearing blood on his beard. Collins could only stare in dumb shock.

"It's actually a good thing you're here, Collins," Tescher said. "You can meet your ski patrollers, the Flying Coyotes. Sunny Valley's finest. We're initiating a new member today and planning our little part in the Karnival parade. This is the first time in years there are actually some skiers up here so we've got to do it right. Boys, this here's Wallace Collins, the man who's buying the mountain out from under us. The man who's finally going to slit Bucky Price's throat and blow up the Lodge. C'mere Lance! Lance is the captain."

Lance, sitting on one of the broken couches, raised a single twisted finger in reply. There were muffled cheers and a bottle skittered across the floor.

"What happened to my son?" Collins said, "I demand to know."

Tescher wobbled and then stepped back. His foot landed on a loose beer bottle and he went down fast, sprawling across the whole floor and roaring with laughter.

"Let's go, Jason," Collins said. "Get Kyle. We'll drive down and find the sheriff in Pine Butte."

"The sheriff? You mean Humphries? I can save you the drive. He'll be here in about a half an hour, soon as he's done getting sucked off by the

Mexican waitresses at the Cattle Guard. H*uh*. He's got them convinced that he's in Immigration."

Jason, with obvious reluctance, helped Kyle off the beer keg he'd been sitting on. Kyle's legs buckled and he would have collapsed but for Jason's arm around his shoulders, steadying him.

"Take it easy, dude," Jason said. He'd guided many a drunken frat brother in his day but this was something different. He felt an acid taste of disgust rise in his throat, disgust at Kyle, at the whole scene. He'd heard Tescher say this was some kind of party, an initiation, but Jason wanted no part of it. "I'll take Kyle outside," Jason said to Wallace Collins. "He's going to need some help."

"No, seriously, Collins." Tescher struggled back to his feet. "There's nothing to get excited about. In fact we did you a big favor. Little Kylie here had an impacted wisdom tooth. Third ventral tricuspid. Bet you didn't know I trained as a dental assistant in the army. It was killing the poor boy."

"You pulled his tooth out?"

"I didn't. I just made the diagnosis."

A shape came forward out of the dark edge of the room. He wore a dog mask, impassive. Collins squinted. "*You*?"

"Huh *huh*. I see you've met. Gavin here is out newest ski patroller, Collins. Our new Flying Coyote. He's done us proud."

"My son has been abused!"

"The poor boy was hurting! It was a humanitarian act on Gavin's part."

Collins heard Kyle vomit behind him, sobbing and wretching. "How in god's name did you pull my son's tooth?"

Gavin held a hand flat out, showing Collins a pair of rubber-handled pliers and a bloody yellow tooth.

"He needed it," Gavin said. "You all bloody need it. Or something like it."

"I've never in my life…"

"You don't like it? Here." Gavin pressed the pliers into Collins's hand. "Get your own back, if you have the guts."

"What are you saying?"

Gavin tilted his mask up, showing his face. He opened his mouth and pushed his jaw forward. "Tek one," he said. "Tek anyone you want, if you can do it."

"You want me to pull out one of your teeth."

"Tek one."

The room fell silent except for Kyle's sobbing in the corner. Collins fingered the pliers in his hand, looking at it like it was a hideous insect. Jason sneezed loudly. Tescher cleared his throat, a booming noise in the small space, but said nothing.

"I won't do it," Collins said finally. "I'm not an animal."

"Then shut up," Gavin said. "You've got plenty to be quiet about. Or do I have to remind you?"

Tescher raised his thick eyebrows. "Huh *huh.* Let's not quarrel. We've got a common interest here, gentlemen. Lots at stake."

"What is this Tescher? Why this violence? I thought we were partners."

"It's your revolution, Collins. You wanted to shake Sunny Valley up. I've tried before but, because of you, this time it's going to happen. Our boy Gavin here proved it can be done. If a few flatlanders get caught up in the party..."--he looked over at Kyle and smiled, showing huge stained teeth—"that's the way it is."

"We are not flatlanders, Tescher. Yes we had an agreement for our mutual benefit. But I see now the kind of people I'm dealing with. I've seen too much. The deal is off. I want my money back."

"You can't back out now, Collins." Tescher wiped a hand across his face. He laughed. "You've opened the gates of hell. Our friend here has drawn the first blood. You're part of it now. Forever."

"What blood? Who are you talking about? My son Kyle? My poor son?"

"Heh heh. We've got a little tradition on our mountain, Collins. If you want to join the Coyotes, you've got to shed some blood. Kill something. Kill something you love..."

Behind them came a triple clicking noise as the door deadbolt turned and turned again. Gavin slipped his mask back over his face and stepped into the darkest corner of the room. The silence became icy as the door opened and a short, broad-shouldered man wearing only a tee shirt and jeans stepped inside.

"Bucky Price," Tescher whispered. "For the love of god.'

A general scramble erupted as the masked creatures stumbled over each other trying to get out the back door. A box of long fluorescent bulbs slid off a shelf, landing on the floor in a series of violent pops.

Tescher turned toward Price, his face weirdly distorted. It was fear, Collins realized. The man was afraid for his life. "Bucky, I can explain," Tescher said. "The Flying Coyotes needed an off-mountain venue for a skier-safety course. We didn't think you'd mind if we…"

"Shut up, Nate. What's wrong with that boy? That's your boy, isn't it Collins?"

Tescher cut in. "Intestinal flu, Bucky. Huh *huh* . We were just arranging to get him down to Pine Butte."

"Don't lie to me Nate. You've been lying to me as long as I've known you and I'm sick of it."

Collins stepped forward. "Mr. Price, perhaps I can…"

Price held a hand up. "Not right now, Mr. Collins. The god's truth is I don't care about any of Tescher's nonsense right now." He squinted around the empty room, sniffed and then grimaced. "The god's truth is I'm looking for my son. He's missing since last night."

"Thad's missing?" Tescher said. "Hear that Collins? Ain't it awful?" He smiled widely. "I dearly hope nothing has happened to him. We all love that boy so much."

Wallace Collins dropped to his knees and held his hands to his eyes.

CHAPTER 19

Darla stood at the big picture window of Tescher's cabin and watched the snow falling in the dark Valley. She was thinking about Stephanie's strange comments about children, about having a daughter, and what it must have been like for Stephanie and her boyfriend to grow up in this isolated place, this lonely, snowy island.

A yellow-orange spark flared up among the dark trees. It lit the surrounding drifts and the falling sheets of snow. The flames below, right down in the village, pulled her attention back to the present. Darla reached along the dark bookcase beside the window and found a pair of binoculars, right where she herself would have kept them. She probably shouldn't be messing with Mr. Tescher's stuff. He was more than a little weird himself.

Darla focused the binoculars but most of the scene was obscured by pine trees. It looked like someone had made a bonfire right in the Lodge parking lot. They'd dumped fuel oil or something else very flammable on it too because the fire was really burning hard, sending flame and sparks high into the sky. Darla wondered if it was part of the Winter Karnival thing she'd been hearing about. It was supposed to start tomorrow. Maybe this was a warm-up event.

Shadows moved around the fire in a ring. Darla could make out people dancing around the blaze and throwing stuff in. Nobody had explained what the heck Karnival was but Darla had assumed it was like the various winter festivals back in New England, with sleigh rides and toboggan races and snow ice cream. What she was seeing was different, though. Something about it just didn't *feel* like a regular old bonfire with hot cocoa and guitars. There was something strange about the people down there, something wrong with their faces, though maybe that was just a distortion from the dark trees and snow.

Darla shivered, wrapped her arms around herself and turned from the window. "Jesus," she said. "Where *is* everybody?" She was freaking herself out with all this stuff about Stephanie and moms and ghost boyfriends. Where was Jason? Where was the big lug when you needed him?

The yellow glow at the window drew Darla back. Jason and her dad had said they were going to get something to eat in the village. They had invited Darla along but she didn't think she could stomach any more of their talk about marketing plans and maximum skier days. Dad and Jason should have been back by now, but there was no movement on what she could see of the road leading up to Tescher's house. The snow was falling steadily, silently, making a thick wall around the Valley. This was Stephanie's world, she thought, this suffocating curtain, this white world. That boy Andy could have been her escape, kind of like like Jason and Bennington College had helped Darla escape from her own depression. But Andy had died, leaving Stephanie behind.

A door slammed downstairs. Darla let her breath out. "Finally!" she called out and then bit her lip. She was happy to have some company but hoped it wasn't Mr. Tescher by himself.

Fast steps came up the wooden stairs. Not Mr. Tescher, then. She looked back down into the valley, at the bonfire and the strange scene around it. She could hear only one set of feet on the stairs. If it was either Dad or Jason, where was the other one?

"Darla! Darla!"

"Dad? I'm over here by the window. Where's Jason?"

Wallace Collins came into the light at the top of the stairs. His thin gray hair was wild on his head—the long stands that he usually combed over his bald spot now stuck out in strange directions. There was a dark stain on the front of his ski bib but his face was pale, unbelievably pale, and his lips were trembling.

"We've must leave immediately, Darla," he said. "Pack some clothes for Kyle and we'll go."

"*Kyle*? I'm not packing anything for Kyle. Where's Jason?"

"Please, no backtalk Darla. Kyle needs our help urgently. He's been injured…brutalized. We're going to leave this place. Where is Tescher?"

"I…I don't know," Darla said. She had never seen her father like this. "He hasn't been here all afternoon."

"I will talk to him. I want you and Jason to take Kyle down to Pine Butte. Down to the doctor there. I will find Teshcer and get my money back. I know he still has the check. I will *make* him give it back to me. It's not too late to do what is right."

"But what *happened*? Was it something to do with the bonfire? Did Kyle fall in or something?"

"What bonfire?"

Darla handed him the binoculars. Collins looked down into the glow of the valley. Another gust of wind whipped open the curtain of snow. "Christ," he said. "God and Christ."

"Isn't that weird? Do they do this every year or something?"

"That's our car they're burning Darla. Our rental car. Kyle and Jason are supposed to be waiting for us there."

CHAPTER 20

"Oh my *god*, April! Look at that guy!"

April squinted out the school bus window. "*Gross.* I mean, could he have, like, any *less* teeth?"

"I bet he gives good blow jobs. Better than you."

"You are *so* gross, Candy."

Numbers spun around and around on the scarred face of a diesel gas pump lit by a weak shop light. Albert reckoned the old bus would clock in at about seventy five dollars and he promised himself a swig of Peppermint Schnapps if he could push it to eighty. The bus driver, a nervous young fellow named Ted, was watching the numbers too, clucking like a mother hen. Albert decided to go easy on him and not spill out too much more than that.

Albert leaned over and spat. "No more'n two of your kids at a time in the store. That's the rule."

Ted smiled like he was on TV. "Don't worry about that, sir. We're from Clemden Bible in Sacramento. It's an evangelical junior college."

"I don't care if all of them just got off the Ark. Only two at a time in the store."

"Yes sir." Ted yelled this information up into the bus and then stood back as twenty or so young people in shiny new ski jackets tumbled off. Every single one—to Albert's amusement—took out their portable telephone, looked at it, frowned, held it to their ear, and then shook it as if the winding drive up Highway 6 had knocked a few parts loose. Pine Butte had no cell phones. Nor was there any higher up.

Albert spat again. The pump was well past the forty dollar mark. This might be worth two sips of Peppermint Schnapps. That Ted fellow seemed nice enough though. He might even be on TV some day, one of those big-money preachers. When Albert spat again he made a point of turning his head slightly to one side, out of respect.

"What brings you folks up here tonight, anyway?" he said. "Highway 6 is closed just another thirty mile up. Closed for winter."

"Oh I know that sir," Ted said. "Excuse me…"

Ted hustled off to a corner of the parking lot where the other young people were standing, ankle deep in slush, waiting to get into the mini mart. One of them, a fat boy in a powder blue snow suit, had slipped and fallen in the snow and four other boys were around him in a circle, pushing and kicking to keep him from getting back up again. Albert grinned, took the nozzle out of the school bus intake and let it run into the snow bank behind the diesel pump. Snow soaks things up real well and he got five or six gallons in there before the young man came back, breathless.

"Can we settle up now?" the young man said. "The students are a little impatient to get going."

"Still fillin' up. You want a full tank if you're going to be driving in the mountains this time of year."

"Gas is quite expensive up here."

"Hee hee. Gracie's got a sign up over there at the mini mart. Sez: 'If you can find a higher price anywhere, we'll match it.' Hee hee." Albert spat. "Where all you folks headed anyway? Nothin but snow further up."

Ted looked surprised. "Isn't this Highway 6? Doesn't this go to Sunny Valley?"

Albert squeezed the nozzle handle and stopped the flow with a loud click. He stood still for a moment, working his chewing tobacco from one cheek to the other.

"Are we full?"

"Not yet." Albert squeezed the nozzle again and the numbers resumed turning. "Going up to Sunny Valley, you say. Tonight?"

"Yes. I mean, no. We're staying at the Woodlands Motel here in Pine Butte tonight and then driving up to Sunny Valley in the morning. Evidently they have some sort of winter carnival on this weekend. I thought it would be a good break for our students."

A bus window lowered and someone pointed a Coke bottle out. They put a thumb over the top and shook. Coke sprayed out, smearing the side of the bus and splattering Ted.

"KELLY," he said, in as low and as stern a voice as he could muster, which wasn't much. Laughter filtered out from inside the bus.

"You've been to this Karnival before, I take it?" Albert said.

Ted wiped his glasses. "No," he said. "I heard about it from the recreation director at our sister school in Presserton, Vermont. Someone on their board of directors recommended it highly."

"Vermont, eh? All sorts of folk from Vermont passing through lately. That's eighty two fifty. Pay inside. Cash or charge only. No checks."

"Gosh. Well, thank you. I'll take care of it and then we'll be on our way."

Albert watched Ted walk quickly toward the mini mart, worriedly counting the cash in his wallet. Another window slid down on the bus and Albert stepped back but this time it was only a cigarette butt, expertly flicked. It landed on the pile of blackened snow that Albert had been soaking with out-of-towner diesel since the plow last came through. He knew it would take more than a cigarette butt to ignite a mound of diesel-soaked snow, but to play it safe he walked over and picked up the smoldering butt. There was lipstick on the filter tip and a good half inch of tobacco left. Albert put it in his mouth, inhaled, and spat it back out again. Menthol. He hated menthol.

Ted jogged back across the parking lot, waved to Albert, and swung up into the school bus. The engine kicked over and, once in gear, the bus headed out of the gas station and onto Highway 6.

Albert watched it go, wondering whether or not he should call the sheriff and let him know just who all was on the way up for tomorrow. He wondered too just how much peppermint schnapps was still in the bottle he had hidden in the recap tires back in the garage. As he watched the bus, two girls stood up in the rear window, bent over and dropped their ski pants, exposing their white behinds.

Albert spat. He would call the sheriff. They were nice behinds. The sheriff would want to know about that.

CHAPTER 21

Darla hurried down the road that wound down from Tescher's house into the village. The deep chill of night had fallen over the Valley and black ice had formed in pockets on the road, invisible. Her father, Wallace Collins, was running ahead, muttering about Kyle. Darla had tried to keep up until she took one heart-stopping slide on the ice. She managed to stay on her feet and not crack her skull on the frozen asphalt, a display of balance worthy of Stephanie Price herself. Darla slowed to a quick but careful walk after that, keeping to the center of the road and away from the darkness of the pines looming on either side.

It was incredibly dark. The lonely, disturbing kind of dark, and Darla felt her old hollow feeling creeping back in. She took a few deep breaths and steadied herself. This was just a broken down old ski village. No one was lost out there in the dark, not her mother, not Stephanie's. She took one more breath and felt better. Normally she loved walking in the snowy woods back in Presserton. But not in the dark.

At the third bend in the road, the last one before the village, Darla smelled the chemical burning of the car. There were voices in the air too, muffled by the trees so it was hard to tell the direction they were coming from. Were Jason and Kyle really down there in the middle of that craziness? Hopefully Jason had the sense to hide someplace, but he might have tried to stop them from burning the car. Jason wasn't much good at being a tough guy. What could have happened to him? And what could Darla do about it?

The road turned into a deep shadow, just the kind of corner that hid the treacherous black ice. Darla walked carefully but after only a few steps she tripped on something and fell sprawling on the ground.

A body. "Dad?"

"Christ damn it."

"Dad? Why are you on the ground?"

"Christ damn it. I slipped. Christ. Help me up."

"It's so icy here. I don't know if I *can* help you up. Can you smell the car burning?"

"Help me up! God, what did I do? My ankle's turned."

"They're *singing* over in that parking lot now. It's so weird. I don't know if we should be going down there."

"Help me up, girl. Kyle's down there."

Darla bent down to try to see her father better in the darkness. He was holding his ankle and his face was twisted in pain. She looked down the dark road, a tunnel of dense looming pines. She could just see one side of the Lodge, lit now by the yellow flicker of the bonfire.

"I'll go," she said. "You wait here until I bring back Jason and Kyle."

"Under no circumstances, Darla. These people are animals. I can't let you go down there alone."

He was interrupted by a growling noise coming through the pine trees, the harsh stutter of a two stroke gasoline engine. Darla turned and stood in front of Collins, facing the woods as if to protect him from whatever was coming.

The angry rattle grew louder. Darla looked for something to use as a weapon but there were only piles of dirty snow, now frozen too hard to even make a snowball. She pulled on a pine branch at her feet but it was half buried in the frozen snow and didn't budge.

"Run and hide, Darla. Hide yourself."

Something was coming out of the darkness. What could it be? Darla really did want to run but she balled her fists, trying to quench her fear. "Don't be stupid, Dad," she said through clenched teeth. "I'm not going to leave you."

"Whatever is coming, it's the devil. That much I know."

The harsh noise surged and then slowed to a rattle, coming close. Darla saw a light, a yellow moving light, and then a snowmobile appeared between the trees.

"Collins?" A stern voice came out of the glare behind the snowmobile headlight.

"That's Bucky Price, Darla."

"What should we do?"

"I don't know."

"Collins? That you there?"

"Yes, Price. I slipped on the snow and perhaps broken my ankle."

The rattling snowmobile shut off and Bucky Price came out of the trees. He wore a camouflage snowsuit, like what Darla had seen hunters wear back in the forests in Vermont. Had he come hunting them?

Price leaned over and felt Collins's ankle with a finger. "Ripped tendons at the very least," he said. "Happens all the time around here with the ice. You'd be surprised how much trouble people can get themselves into just walking around."

"Please, Mr. Price," Collins said, "I must find my son."

"Let's get you and the lady up on the Ski-doo. I was coming looking for you anyway. Tescher's down there in the parking lot with his boys. I figured you'd see the fire and wonder what was going on. I wanted to head you off before you got into any more trouble."

"Tescher? I must see him. He has…he has something that belongs to me. And my son. We must find my son."

"Don't worry Collins. It's all under control."

With Darla under one shoulder and Bucky Price under the other they moved Wallace Collins cautiously onto the snowmobile.

"You get on too, Darling."

"That's *Darla*, Mr. Price.

"Yes ma'am. We can all fit on if we squeeze together. I wouldn't want to leave you out here for the Coyotes."

Before Darla could reply, Price fired up the snowmobile, drowning out any further conversation. It started with a lurch and Darla heard her father moan with pain.

CHAPTER 22

"Andy? Andy. "

I wasn't hiding. I was sitting in one of the comfortable chairs in the lounge reading tomorrow's assignment for English Literature. I was in the college prep class, which meant that a special teacher drove up to Pine Butte High School twice a week to teach us about meter and feet, stanzas and rhyme schemes, Gothics and Beats.

"*Andy.*"

The teacher, Miss Bell, was a graduate of UOP down in Stockon and seemed to be not much older than the rest of us. She was obsessed by the wild, romantic poetry of the Brontë sisters. When reading their poetry aloud she would sit on a stool at the center of class and let her long black hair fall in a curtain over her face. Stephanie hated Miss. Bell but I didn't care. The words would emerge like late winds out of the valley and howl and swirl around me until I lost what little direction I had.

> *Alone I sat; the winter day*
> *Had died in smiling light away*
> *I saw it die, I watched it fade*
> *From snowy hill and frosty glade*

"Andy! For god's sake what are you doing here?"

"My homework," I said calmly. "Those college tests are next month. I want to be ready."

"Well I'll be. And the rooms? We had twelve checkouts today. You take care of that first. Carlie can wash the sheets and towels tonight during her shift. That'll save you time."

"No."

Bucky put his hands to his waist and stood up a little straighter, calling himself to attention as it were. At that same moment a guest couple crossed the lounge. They were dressed for an evening in the Lodge dining room and bar. Both had the raccoon-mask sunburn that comes from a day's skiing in goggles.

"Will we see you later, Bucky?" the woman said, stopping to put her hand on his shoulder.

"You betcha. You folks enjoy your dinner and we'll meet later."

She laughed, a sound like icicles hitting the sidewalk, and they walked away.

"Andy."

"Stephanie says this is more important," I said.

"Come here."

I put my books to one side. This was the start. I stood up and moved to the center of the room. He circled me like a staff sergeant inspecting a new recruit. He brought his nose so close to my mouth that I could have bit it off. He sniffed.

"Have you been drinking?"

"No."

"Why do I smell cigarettes?"

"Thad drove me home from school," I said.

"My son does not smoke."

I said nothing. There was no chance that Thad was going get into trouble over smoking and I had made my point.

"That's enough of this nonsense, Andy. Get up there and knock off those rooms. You've got plenty of time after dinner to read your books."

"Stephanie said…"

The slap came at lightning speed and I wasn't prepared. One moment I was standing up to Bucky, facing him, the next I was on the pine plank floor of the lounge with the side of my face stinging like I had been dragged across the snow for miles. I could hear nothing at first, only Miss Bell's voice in my head.

> Rolled round with goodly loam and cradled deep,
> These bone shanks will not wake immaculate
> To trumpet-toppling dawn of doomstruck day :
> They loll forever in colossal sleep;

Nor can God's stern, shocked angels cry them up
From their fond, final, infamous decay.

Finally it cleared. Looking up, I saw Bucky standing over me, his fists clenched, breathing as if he'd run six miles. He hadn't, of course. He was angry. He'd lost his temper. I smiled, stood up and walked toward the back of the lounge, toward the service door.

Outside on the icy flat behind the Lodge, Bucky and I squared off just behind the bear-proof dumpsters. He had Army training. I was taller, with a longer reach, and I'd been studying Gibson's *Art and Science of Boxing* for the past week. I'd even picked a few fights with Pine Butte boys just to practice my skills.

I led with my left hand and circled, jabbing toward his strong side. Bucky, looking amused, put his hands up too, ready to box.

"They teach you how to fight in that poetry class of yours?" he said.

I reached in with my left and tried to punch with my right, aiming at his jaw, but he swatted my hand away like it was a horsefly. Before I could react his right flashed out. I dodged back but not before his knuckles caught my lips, slicing them open against my teeth. I spat blood onto the snow.

"Why don't we get back to work, Andy?" He was not breathing hard, where I was bent over, puffing great clouds of steam.

"No." I straightened.

"Since when are you a troublemaker? I'm going down to that school tomorrow and find out what they're teaching you."

"Stephanie said..."

Again the blow came fast and aimed for my head. He caught my cheekbone and for a moment the world flashed yellow. If he'd followed up with a jab to my throat I would have been dead. But he didn't. He just stood glaring at me, puffing slightly, his eyes the color of a burning forest. My face was torn with pain now, but not so much that I hadn't seen and understood what happened. Stephanie's name always drew a full round-house from Bucky. And not only that: he dropped his left. I had learned what the *Art and Science of Boxing* said I should learn by sparring with my opponent, but it wasn't enough. He was too fast, too strong.

I lowered my fists and wiped my face on my shirt, which was damp with cold sweat. Then I turned and walked back inside.

Bucky followed me as I walked to the cleaning closet and took out my mop and bucket. I put them on the cleaning cart along with the toilet brush, the dust rags and the sponges. I could hear Bucky breathing behind me, but I knew there was nothing more he could do.

"My daughter," he said finally. His voice came out as if squeezed between two boulders. "I know all about you two. I know everything. I want you to leave her alone. You're not to talk to her, you're not to be alone together. Is that understood?"

I pushed the cart along the hallway. There were guests everywhere, showered and changed, some already with drinks in hand. Bucky couldn't touch me, couldn't say anything, only follow in a blind rage.

The service elevator only held the cleaning cart and one person. I pushed the button, got in, and closed the door behind me. Through the wire-meshed window I saw Bucky still standing, fuming, outside. I hit the button for the third floor and rose out of sight. I'd given him a chance. He could have killed me with a single punch after that shot to my cheek. But he didn't. He had his chance. Now it was my turn.

CHAPTER 23

From what Darla could see, the snowmobile was driving through a dark spider's web. Pine branches crossed crazily in front of them, lit only by glances of moonlight. The snow underneath was mottled by shadow. Bucky Price seemed to know the route well. He maneuvered his snowmobile skillfully between the trees, finding lanes that were invisible to Darla and Wallace Collins and avoiding the densest pine growth. They only had to duck a few times.

The noise of the snowmobile made conversation impossible, but just when Darla was feeling truly confused about where they were going, they turned into a clearing behind the Lodge. It was a service area strewn with rusted barrels and broken furniture. Price had evidently steered them in a huge circle through the trees so that they could get to the Lodge and avoid the mad scene in the parking lot—their burning SUV and the shapes dancing around it.

"Price, can we please…"

Bucky Price held out a gloved hand. "One minute," he said in a quiet voice. He pulled a bundle of keys from inside his snow suit and unlocked a steel door in the side of the Lodge. Darla was surprised to see stairs inside, heading down into a basement room. "Please go in," he said. "It's the safest place right now."

"I want to see my son," Collins said.

"And Jason!" Darla said, "Where is Jason?"

"They're already inside. Please go in. I'll run upstairs and get the first aid kit so we can splint that ankle, Collins. I won't be a minute."

Price pushed the door open. Collins, with his arm around Darla's shoulders, limped inside. As they stepped together through the door, Darla felt a stifling blast of hot air. Her eyes watered over and she could see almost nothing except the harsh light of bare fluorescent bulbs overhead.

"Squeaker!"

It was Jason. He ran up to help Collins down the stairs and then hugged Darla tightly. "You okay, Squeaker?" he said. "Mr. Collins? What happened? Did they attack you too? You can sit down over here." Jason cleared some jackets and ski pants off a wooden chair in the corner and carried it to the center of the room.

"Calm down, Jason." Darla said. "He just sprained his ankle. We're okay."

"Where is Kyle? Where is my son?"

Jason looked up at Darla and winced. He nodded toward a military cot in the corner. "He's asleep," he said.

"Asleep! At a time like this?"

Jason held Darla's gaze and tapped his forearm significantly. Darla mouthed the word 'Oh". "He's had a hard day, Mr. Collins," Jason said. "Those Coyote guys followed us down to the parking lot. We got in the car but they surrounded it and smashed the windows. Mr. Price and Stephanie showed up right then. I was scared to death but they walked through that crowd like they weren't even there. That guy Tescher just stood like he was made of stone."

"He's an animal, that man. An animal. To think he has my check for a half million dollars. What they did to Kyle…"

"Yeah, well, all the Coyotes just stood back while Price got us out of the car. Stephanie led us down here while he took off on his snowmobile to find you guys."

Darla looked around. "Where *is* Stephanie?"

"I dunno. She opened the door and then we had to stand outside while she went in. I thought she was just checking it out but I'm pretty sure she grabbed some stuff. Then we went in and she locked the door behind us."

The room was so hot that Darla was already sweating. She shrugged off her jacket and looked around. The walls were concrete block and the room was barely fifteen feet square. A large gas-fired furnace and two huge hot water heaters took up the far side of the room—heat and hot water for the whole Lodge, she supposed—with bulky pipes leading out of them, criss-crossing awkwardly up into the ceiling. No wonder it was so hot in here. In the opposite corner was a green folding cot where Kyle lay sleeping and the overstuffed chair where Wallace Collins sat, holding his ankle uncomfortably. There were a few wooden packing crates stacked up as if to act as shelves, and a small desk with a row of three drawers down one side.

Jason hugged her. "You doin' okay Squeaker? I'm here for ya. Don't be scared."

Darla said nothing. She wasn't particularly scared, she realized. She'd stood up to the darkness back on the forest road and nothing bad had happened besides a wild ride on Mr. Price's snowmobile. Maybe she was finally getting over the darkness thing.

Darla opened her eyes and examined the concrete wall behind Jason's shoulder. Unlike the other walls in the room, this one was covered with stuff, but she couldn't recognize immediately what it was. Peeling paint or wallpaper? Who would wallpaper this awful room?

"It's all Stephanie," Darla said suddenly.

"What?"

"This wall. Look behind you. These are all old newspaper clippings that someone put up here with scotch tape. See? And they're all about Stephanie Price."

Wallace Collins twisted around in his chair. "I can't see that far."

Darla unwound herself from Jason's bear hug and walked slowly to the wall. She touched one yellowed strip after another. "Her whole life is up here. See? She's about seven years old in this one. She won some ski race. I didn't know kids that young could race."

"Pre-juniors," Collins said. "The big ski areas have it. I'm surprised they had enough skiers here."

"What's amazing is, I mean look at her face. She looks almost the same as she does now. Don't you think, Jason?"

"I dunno. I never actually saw her."

"Here, see? This one's from a few years ago when she was leaving for the Olympic training camp. She's standing in front of those big chainsaw bears in the lounge. There's Mr. Price and Mr. Tescher."

"Price and Tescher together?" said Wallace Collins. "When was *that* taken?"

Jason sniffed and put his face closer to the wall. "Five years ago," he said. "She does look just like she did as a little kid. Some things have sure changed, though."

Darla elbowed Jason out of the way. "You're such a pig, sometimes." She scanned the rest of the wall. "That's kind of the end of the story. You've got all these clippings of her winning races and trophies all over the place—oops, here's one where she's reading poetry or something—and then it's like high school and the Olympic training camp and then that's it. I wonder why Mr. Price..."

The steel door slammed overhead. Price descended the stairs, now dressed in Levis and a white tee shirt. The shirt emphasized his skin, rough and deeply tanned, and his thick arms and chest.

Price surveyed the room, looking over the cot, the shelves, the desk, the wall of newspaper clippings. His eyes lingered on each item, ignoring everyone in front of him. Darla felt he was looking right through them into other time. Deep sadness grew into dark lines on his face. He has lost something in his life, Darla thought. Something precious. His wife? No one ever talked about Caroline, Stephanie's mother, the previous owner of Sunny Valley.

"I've helped you Collins," Bucky Price said. His voice was distant at first, then grew steady. "You're safe here. But you need to help me or none of us will be safe for long. Collins, I know you've had dealings with someone in Sunny Valley. I want you to tell me who it is."

"You mean Tescher? There's no secret there. I intended to buy the Ski Center and his lease on the mountain. But I'm pulling out of that deal. You must help me find him so I can recover my money."

"Not Tescher." Price seemed unsteady on his feet. "My son Thad is missing. Now Stephanie has disappeared. We had good snow this season but Tescher's men are stirred up like they haven't been for years. In some ways I'm grateful to you Collins. You've woken me up. I see now that something is changing here. Something inside us."

"I'm sorry, Price. I know we are out-of-towners, but I didn't realize my interest would disrupt the community so drastically."

"It's not you, Collins," Bucky Price said. He scanned his eyes around the room, looking from wall to wall. "It's not you. But I think you know who it is."

CHAPTER 24

I escaped to the ridge every Saturday for the rest of that season. Stephanie joined me on the weekends she wasn't racing. She taught me technique, especially the difficult weight shift required on Telemark skis. She also showed me how to read the terrain. All of my skiing so far had been at Tescher's Ski Center, where the runs were smoothed and flattened every night by grooming machines. The runs were rated green, blue or black, but it only took a year or two of regular skiing for me to know all the runs well.

Here on the ridge, I learned, conditions could change from day to day, hour to hour. A single night's snowfall with a westerly wind put a steep overhanging lip onto the central bowl, turning an easy wide-open run into a groin-chilling drop. A few hours in the sun would then turn the over-hang into a cosmic hammer, tons of snow waiting to release down the mountain at just the wrong moment.

Stephanie knew well how to read the slopes and conditions, though she couldn't always explain her knowledge clearly.

"Just stand here for a minute," she said one day as we reached the top of the lip. I didn't know it then but it would be our last Saturday together. "*Listen* to the snow. Pick some up and feel it in your hand. It's deadly. Can't you tell? It can't *wait* to let go."

I said nothing. The Sierra sun was blue and perfect overhead. The ridgeline trees—junipers mostly—were covered in fresh snow. The scene was idyllic, picturesque. Twice that season, we had seen sections of the cornice release, turning the slope into a thundering river of ice blocks and snow, but I still thought of it as a curiosity. Death seemed far away.

"I'll ski it," I said. "I'm not scared."

"You will not. I'm not done with you yet."

Later, after we'd finished our runs, we lay on the ridgetop and warmed in the sun. Stephanie's hands cupped my ears, warming them. Her fingers explored the channels and lobes. Her thumbs worked up my skull, feeling it, probing it, as if looking for sensitive spots, for weakness.

I lay with my head in her lap, limbs stretched out, afternoon sun full on my face. I had learned to bring a fleece blanket in my backpack for our trips up the ridge, so I was comfortable. Her touch, the feel of her wet lips on my forehead, the small sighs that passed through her from moment to moment put me in real heaven. We'd taken three runs down the back of the bowl, each one steeper, wilder, closer to that heart-stopping moment of disaster. Then we made salty, sweaty love on the ridge until skiing and loving were one thing, an endless falling, a perfect weightlessness, a disappearance of sun, sky, self.

"Speak something," she said, fingers hot on my temples.

"I can't. I really can't." It was true. I was as empty as the sky. "You do it."

Stephanie inhaled.

> *When, in disgrace with Fortune and men's eyes*
> *I alone beweep my outcast state*
> *And trouble deaf heaven with my bootless cries*
> *And look upon myself and curse my fate*

"Stop it," I said. "It's not funny."

She squeezed my head in her arms. I felt her lips liquid on my eyelids. She laughed. "That sonnet SO makes me think of you. The poor little orphan boy cast out by fate, rescued by strangers. It's romantic."

She was trying to rile me but I wasn't going to let it happen. Stephanie needed me now as much as I needed her. If I was lost, desperate, hopeless, then so was she. I took a deep breath and let my mind slip open. Words flowed in. "Two can play the Shakespeare game," I said. I closed my eyes and spoke:

> *My mistress' eyes are nothing like the sun*
> *Coral is far more red than her lips red*
> *If snow be white, why then her breasts are dun*
> *If hairs be wires, black wires grow on her head*

"Very funny. I'm blond, in case you hadn't noticed."

"Thy breasts are pretty dun, though," I said, reaching up to touch her thermal shirt. She slapped my hand a way.

"You're such a jerk sometimes." She squeezed her arms together until my head was locked. As always I could feel her heat through her clothes. "When are you going to do it?" she said.

"Do what?"

She squeezed tighter. Her fingers reached into the neck of my tee shirt and found the bones of my windpipe, stroking them. "You know what. When are you going to do it? There's only a month left until selection. I want you to do it over Karnival."

"Kiss me," I said. "Why Karnival?"

"It's a secret." She leaned forward and put her tongue hot into my mouth. She unwound her arms and now her hands were on my face, her thumbs near my eye sockets. We could never just kiss—we could only pour into each other, rip each other open to find something that had been lost a very long time. She took my other hand in her mouth and bit the flesh at the base of my palm. I sat up, rubbing my hand. There were white marks but no blood.

"It's not going to be a fair fight," I said. "He's too good."

"I don't care about that. That's why you should poison him. Rat poison or something. Do it over Karnival. No one will ever suspect."

I laughed and shook my head. "I don't think there's enough rat poison in the maintenance closet to kill Bucky. Why do you want me to kill him over Karnival?"

"If I tell you the secret, will you do it? How about a gun? Can't you get a gun someplace? Thad has a hunting rifle. Use that."

"A secret? You don't have any secrets from me."

"I do, though. When are you going to do it?"

"Be patient," I said. "I have to do it right or I'll end up in jail."

Stephanie sat up and began putting on her ski boots. "Who cares," she said. "I'm already *in* jail."

CHAPTER 25

Bucky Price knelt to tape Wallace Collins's leg into a foam splint.

"I don't know what you're talking about, Price," Collins said. "I have no more interest here. I'm going to get my money back and then we are leaving for ever."

"I think you do know what I'm talking about, Collins, but maybe we're both finding it hard to accept. Hard to understand what we've done."

Bucky Price's voice was stern but, again, Darla thought it was only a shell, an act he was putting on for them. The deep sorrowful lines in his face showed that he was under some unbearable weight.

Darla swallowed. "We were just admiring your collection of clippings," she said, trying to break the painful tension in the room. "All those photos of your lovely daughter. It's so sweet of you to keep them all."

Price came forward and put one of his dark hands to the wall, touching the clippings with calloused fingers. He turned around quickly. "These aren't mine," he said. "These belonged to my foster son, Andy. This was his bedroom."

"Somebody *lived* down here?"

"Andy liked it. Of course he had free heat all winter long."

"I had no idea you had another son, Price."

Bucky Price inhaled deeply. "Foster son, Collins. Foster son. A charity case. A service to the state of California."

"I guess he doesn't live in Sunny Valley anymore," Collins said. "We would have met him."

There was a long silence. "Unfortunately the young man is dead. He was the victim of an avalanche five years ago. The same avalanche that crippled Thad."

Darla looked at Price's deeply creased forehead. "I'm so sorry," she said. "I heard about it. It must have been a terrible loss for you."

"It was," Price said. "And not just for me. For this whole community. Sunny Valley. Thad was skiing at an international level at that time. He had corporate sponsorships and endorsements. Warren Miller had plans to come to Sunny Valley the following season. He cancelled after Thad was injured."

A raspy voice came out of the corner of the room. "You mean the ski movie dude?"

Everyone turned. Kyle was awake. He stood up unsteadily, took a few steps, and then sat down on the desk at the back of the room. His black mop of hair swirled crazily around his head, but he had changed his shirt and looked better than he had a few hours earlier.

Wallace Collins limped across the room and stood in front of his son.

"Open your mouth," he said.

"Forget it dad."

"Open your mouth, son. I want to Price to see what those animals did to you."

"Dad, just fucking forget it. I'm okay."

"Don't use that language with me."

Kyle didn't reply but instead bent down and started to open and close the drawers on the desk, one at a time, ignoring his father.

"*Kyle.*"

"Please Mr. Collins," said Bucky Price. His hands were on his hips. The sadness in his face was dissolving. "I'm not sure how much time we have."

Collins turned. "You can begin by telling me what we're doing here. Why are we imprisoned in this room? I demand to use the telephone. I want to call the police and get medical attention for my son."

"Can we go upstairs?" said Darla. "It's *so* hot in here."

Price walked to the center of the room and began to pace. He ran his fingers through his short military-style hair. Suddenly he stopped, standing nearly at attention in the center of the room.

"As I said, it's for your own safety. I can't have you in the Lodge where you might be seen from outside. After Karnival is over, we'll see."

"What *is* Karnival?" Darla said. "I keep hearing about it but no one's told me what it really is. What's so dangerous about Karnival that we have to hide down here? Isn't it just a winter festival or something?"

Price remained silent in the middle of the room. Nothing moved but a vein throbbing in his forehead. Darla watched his face grow red. Something was building up inside.

"It was, at one point," he said.

The words barely escaped through his lips.

CHAPTER 26

Stephanie faced me and sat back on her heels. It was like story time at the Pine Butte library, but she wasn't smiling inanely like the librarian used to.

"Did you ever hear about Candle Night? Did anyone ever mention it?"

"No." I sat cross-legged on the blanket, wondering what new part of my own world was about to open up in front of me.

"I guess not. It stopped before you came here. Mama was *so* angry. She told me so."

I said nothing, but remembered the tall woman, the long white shape. Already we were on forbidden ground. I had been beaten for asking about Mrs. Price.

"Candle Night was this old thing. Mama said they did it in the Valley when she was a little girl. All the high mountain people came to their cabin, even the Washoe Indians. She said the only time Granpa Igmar would allow Indians into the Valley was Candle Night."

Stephanie closed her eyes and rocked back. Her mouth opened slightly to the sky, as if she was about to recite some poetry. "I was pretty little when we used to do it but I remember. I remember. The cabin was still there. Daddy hadn't built the Lodge yet. He built it right on top of the old cabin. Did you know Mama's parents are buried under the big stone fireplace in the lounge? Granpa Igmar and Granma Sophie?"

"That's weird."

"Daddy didn't like them, but they wanted to be buried near the old cabin. He couldn't refuse."

"So?"

"Okay, so what I remember is this would happen in January. When the snow was the deepest. Everyone gathered in the front room of the cabin late at night. The table was piled with any sort of food that people had around their cabins. Sacks of pine seeds, acorn flour, mountain honey. Sometimes a butchered deer. But no one would eat or drink. Mama turned the lanterns down and then one of the old Indians would walk through the room with a candle. He smelled like dogs and sagebrush. All the women and girls—Mama included—held a candle and he would light each one. And then *I* followed behind him." Stephanie's eyes closed and she shook her hair back. She looked like a very young girl, the age when I first saw her. "I carried a little pot of honey. Each woman would lift her shirt and I would touch her stomach with my fingers and rub some honey on it."

"*That's* weird," I said.

"It wasn't weird. You're just ignorant. It's what people used to do around here. After me and the old Indian had gone around the circle, the men would carry the table with all the food outside onto the snow. They'd pour kerosene on it and set it all on fire. Everything. The food, the table, everything."

"This is all bullshit."

"I swear it's true. I know it's true because Mama told me never to tell anyone. I sang too. Mama taught me how to sing when I was teeny tiny." Stephanie took a deep breath, leveled her head and fixed her gaze in the distance. I could hear nothing at first, but slowly her voice built to an uneven moan, a two-pitched sound that wound in and out. "Ah-a la la la. Ah-a la la la." The sound grew and shrank, finally becoming a whispering coo, the sound of a Snowy Owl.

Stephanie's eyes had turned violet, a color I had seen only once before, the first time we made love on the ridge. I remembered how cold I was that day, how afraid. "Why you?" I said. "Why were you the one going around touching people's bellies and singing? Were there other kids there?'

"No. Only me. Of course it was me! I'm the sixth! Mama was the fifth. Who else would do it?"

"I don't know. What does that mean, the sixth?"

Stephanie stood up. The lesson was over. "They couldn't have Candle Night without me." She said. "I was the special girl. Mama said so."

CHAPTER 27

Bucky Price stood in the middle of the concrete block room. His face had hardened. The lines of pain and loss that Darla had seen earlier were now engraved in stone.

"I built this Lodge after I finished my second tour of duty in Vietnam," he said. "Tescher served a few years longer than I did but when he came back I loaned him some money and gave him a hundred year lease on the mountain."

"A *transferable* lease, Price. Why did you do that? It was bound to cause problems."

Price folded his arms behind his back and marched thoughtfully across the room. "I didn't know better at the time, Collins. A lawyer recommended it, said it would make the deal more attractive to Tescher. It was a family matter. I'm sure you understand."

"Family is important to me too, Price. That is why I demand you release us. My son needs medical attention."

"Tescher took my money and the mountain," Price said, ignoring Collins. "We were partners. Our futures were tied together."

Darla felt a swirling in her head suddenly clarify. "And the past! Mr. Tescher told me about it that first night we were here. When we were driving in his car. Wasn't Mr. Tescher's great great grandfather the original settler here? Isn't that his picture in the lobby with the Indian girl?"

"Darla," Wallace Collins said, "We're trying to have a serious discussion here."

"Yes, Darla," Price cut in, "it's true, though it hardly matters. I'm not even sure to what extent Igmar Tescher really was related to Cor Tescher, the original settler of Sunny Valley. Igmar came to Sunny Valley as a ranch hand. He might have heard some local history and got it in his head that he was owed something. But you asked about Karnival. Please let me finish."

"Okay," Darla said. She chewed her lip a little and then stopped herself.

"Highway 6 closes at the summit in winter. Back when Tescher and I first opened the mountain, most flatlanders didn't even know Sunny Valley was here. I wanted something special to attract folks in mid winter. The locals used to all get together in January, a kind of party to hope for better times. I thought we could do something like that. Nothing out of the ordinary, you understand. Tescher would have some ski races and sled rides. I'd decorate the Lodge and bring up a piano player from Reno. I saw once on television how Disneyland had a nighttime parade so we planned something like that too. And I tell you what, for ten years our Karnival was the most popular..."

A muffled explosion interrupted Price's story. The steel door shook and made an odd pop and crackle noise.

"Buckshot," said Price, setting his lower lip. "I should go out there before things get out of hand."

"Sounds to me like the situation is already out of hand, Price," Wallace Collins said.

Price ignored him. "I'll get to the point and we'll see if we can help each other. After Thad and that unfortunate young man—" he nodded toward the wall of newspaper clippings—"had their accident, certain folks in this town got ideas. Bad ideas. For some reason they blamed the whole sad event on me. To make matters worse, that storm, the avalanche storm, turned out to be the last real snow we were going to get around here for a fair few years. A drought took hold like no one had ever seen. Sunny Valley got almost no snow four seasons in a row. Tescher bought some snow making equipment but he couldn't afford to cover hardly any of the mountain. It broke him, finally. That's how he ended up talking to you, Collins."

"I'd assumed some such."

"I understood about folks being angry," Price said. "But they blamed me—my family—for everything. For the avalanche, the drought, for Tescher's going broke."

"Your fault, Price? How could you have caused an avalanche? Or a drought?"

"Maybe we aren't as smart up here as other people. We used to have all kinds of guests come stay in the Lodge and ski—movie stars, politicians, Olympic athletes. But come Sunday night all those smart folk drove back down the hill and it's just us waiting out the long nights of the week, trying to stay warm because the heaters are turned off to save money. We here in the Valley have to get through the nights, get through the season, and not talk each other crazy. After the flatlanders stopped coming it got even harder."

Something heavy pounded irregularly against the outer door. Everyone except Price looked over, wondering how strong the door really was.

"That first dry winter, that dead winter with Thad still in the hospital down the hill, folks got it in their mind to turn Karnival back into the old tradition. An offering for better times."

"They were praying for snow?" Darla said.

"Yes, I guess they were. That year, after the parade Tescher's boys built a bonfire right in my parking lot. They made up a dummy out of some old clothes that I guess was supposed to be me. I tried to stop them—there were a few folk staying in the Lodge, even with no snow— but it got wild. That was when the back wing burned. I was lucky the whole Lodge didn't go."

More banging at the door and muffled voices. Price didn't look concerned. He set his face into a frown as if he was watching some unruly children. "To be honest, I don't know what's going to happen this year. We've got good snow on the ground, so tomorrow folk'll drive up from the flatland and ski and drink cocoa and get their mittens wet. Tescher'll put on a ski race and one of the local boys will win and he'll pick a fight with a boy from Pine Butte. We'll have the parade at five o'clock." Price looked at his hands. "But after that I'm going to make sure all those folks get in their cars and go back down the mountain. Because after night falls the ski patrol boys will go out on the highway and block off the road with cones. Then the real Karnival will start." Price took a deep breath. "It's not about snow anymore. We've got good snow. It's not even about me.

They don't bother making an effigy."

"What *is* it about?"

"Collins, I'm trying to explain to you what we are up against. I'll say it for the last time. I need to know who you were talking to before you came to Sunny Valley. Who brought you here? How did you find us? Was it Stephanie?"

Collins shook his head slowly. "No one," he said, his lips barely moving. "There was no one."

The door shuddered under heavy blows.

"I've got to go. You folks are fine for the moment. But Collins, remember: I'm the only person up here who can guarantee your safety."

"You're going out there Price? Someone's got an axe or a hammer. There was gunfire earlier. You'll be killed."

Price smiled. A chill ran down Darla's spine. It was exactly Stephanie's hollow smile, the one that made Darla feel like she was from another planet. "I'm in no danger," Price said. "We still have power here. Remember, those folk out there think we brought down the avalanche and caused the drought." Again, the hollow smile. "They think we dried up heaven."

CHAPTER 28

Nate Tescher stopped, leaned on his ski poles and looked up along the dark slope ahead of him. It had been twenty years since he'd last strapped on skis and skins to climb Little Spring Ridge and he was feeling it. He gasped for breath and the night air seared his lungs. His mouth tasted like sour milk. He spat into the well of a blue fir.

Tescher wiped his face and started upward again, following a small glow bobbing up the ridge a hundred yards ahead. He snorted. She was stupid to carry a light when the whole slope was lit by the moon. Anyone could follow her. And there were tracks, of course. Tescher stopped again to catch his breath and look down at Stephanie's tracks in the snow. She was so light that even when kicking into the steep and icy sections she barely broke the crust. But she made tracks, all right. Forget that witch magic crap. Everybody made tracks.

Tescher took off his flannel shirt, wrapped it around his waist, and continued moving upward, his breath loud in his own ears. He'd worried at first that she would hear him gasping and hawking his way up but she'd pulled far enough ahead now that it probably didn't matter.

And the stupid bitch was singing. Wavering, uneven notes floated down the slope like spring snow. The song surrounded Tescher and made him kick harder into the snowy face and dig deeper into his gut for the energy to keep going. He'd heard that song nearly all his life. He hated it.

The light stopped ahead. Stephanie had paused right below the steep chute under the ridge. Tescher laughed and spat again. She was resting. He wasn't the only person around here who'd lost something in the last few years. Miss Big Time Olympic Skier, first alternate in downhill and G.S., darling of the Sierra. She was probably puking her guts out up there.

Tescher gripped his poles, planted them hard, and kicked into the snow.

There had been a time when he'd climbed this slope nearly every day, usually with a cigarette in his mouth and a nasty hangover in his head. The idea made Tescher want to laugh but he dared not. Stephanie was still at the ridgeline and he'd drawn much closer. Back when Bucky Price was still just a ranch hand in the Valley, they would race to the top on heavy wooden skis with genuine seal skins stuck to the bottom with bee's wax. The rules of the race were simple: there were no rules. Price once kicked Tescher in the head right at the chute where Stephanie was holding now. The ski edge sliced Tescher's scalp open and his blood poured onto the snow in a river. Price had gone on to claim the ridge before dropping back to bandage Tescher and help him down. Tescher never held it against him—not that—even though for the ten minutes he'd sat holding handfuls of snow against his forehead and watching his own red blood pour down his arms, Tescher had been convinced he would die.

They were young fools then. He and Price nearly killed themselves on this ridge during their last year of high school and for no good reason. Vietnam was on and they were sure they were going to be drafted. Price's father had been part of the famous 10th Mountain Division in World War II, the division trained for fighting in the European Alps. Bucky figured if they volunteered for the 10th Mountain, as his father had, they could spend the war skiing in Colorado instead of sweating in the jungle. It wasn't until they'd signed their papers down in Pine Butte that the recruiter told them that the 10th Mountain had been dissolved after the war. Tescher ended up on a medical post in Korea. Price had gone into the jungle with the 1st Cavalry.

The light ahead winked twice and then disappeared. She'd finally got up the strength for the final push to the ridge. She wasn't far away, though. Tescher could still hear the song. It seemed to come from every direction and hadn't stopped for even a moment while she'd been catching her breath.

Tescher spat. He'd come up here with his sister Caroline after old Igmar died, just before he shipped out for Basic. She sang that same song and promised Tescher that this time, this generation, things would be different. They'd forget all that female bloodline crap and Sunny Valley would be his. It would stay with the Tescher name, the Tescher blood, the rightful owners who had won the Valley in the first place. But when Tescher finished his tour (plus two years in the brig for assault) and came back home, Caroline had married Bucky Price.

On that first night back from 'Nam, Tescher pounded on the door of the old cabin with a stick of firewood and finally smashed a window. The log door opened but Bucky—a skilled jungle assassin with a silver star to prove it—didn't come out into the starless night. Caroline did, her eyes red, her face flushed and pale. "Turned out there weren't no choice about it," she said to Tescher. "There's more to the Valley than just a lot of old trees and snow. You know that anyway, Nate. But Bucky will see you right."

"I'll kill him first," Tescher said.

"You won't, neither. He's going to build a big lodge, bring the rich folk here. He wants you to set up a ski mountain."

"That costs money."

She put one hand on the back of Tescher's neck and a thumb to his forehead and began to sing. She sang the song and Tescher's anger turned into something deeper but much further away. He was alone now in this frozen, hollow world. His parents were dead, buried beside the cabin. His sister had abandoned him. His best friend had betrayed him. A cold white wind stirred up suddenly around Tescher and Caroline and his mind turned blank, keeping only enough consciousness to wonder if Price had a sniper rifle trained on him through the broken window of the cabin. "He'll loan you the money, Nate."

"That's my money."

"You just build that ski mountain. You'll get money of your own."

"What about you?"

Caroline tightened her hands and blew lightly around his ears and scalp. "I don't have much time," she said. "You know that. We women here, we never have much time."

The next day bulldozers arrived and smashed the Tescher family cabin to matchsticks. The blanched white crosses next door were taken away and the new foundation was staked out: a three-foot concrete slab to be poured over the heads of old Igmar and Sophie.

"It'll bring good luck," Price had said about building a ski lodge on top of Tescher graves. Tescher could only spit in response.

The Price and Caroline lived in a canvas tent while the Lodge was built. Tescher, who'd been sleeping in his truck, moved into his father's old house and accepted a check from Bucky Price for more money than he thought existed in the whole world.

Chapter 29

There I am clearly. My hair is sand-colored and coarse. I can barely pull a comb through it when it gets long so I keep it short. I cut my hair myself once a week with scissors I stole from the front desk.

My face is strange, even to me. I have a large forehead and a sharp nose. My neck is endless, like a giraffe's. My lips are rough, burnt by sun and wind. Spots litter my face, large freckles that turn nearly black in the sun. Bucky Price calls them devil spots. He would know.

How can she love me? How can anyone?

I spray ammonia across the mirror and watch myself disappear in the fog. I'm changing, I think. I'm in a cocoon and when it opens I'll be a different person. I take a paper towel off the roll and wipe the mirror. I start in one corner where there is only light reflected from the overhead fluorescent fixture. I clean the corners, the edges, the top and sides of the mirror, leaving only my outline smeared and unclear. Today is the day. I will kill Bucky Price and wipe away the fog. I will claim Stephanie and Sunny Valley as my own. I will know who I am.

I reach inside my flannel shirt and pull out a new knife in its sheath. I bought it two weeks ago at Barley's Hardware in Pine Butte, along with the gray whetstone I've used every night to sharpen the edge into a razor. I slide the knife from its sheath and look again into the mirror, the smeared, obscure glass. I move my arm in a broad sweep. The knife gleams clearly, the image reflects perfectly.

A knife in the side of the throat is my best chance. I learned that from one of Bucky's own Army Ranger manuals found in a box in my basement room. One stroke. If it doesn't break his windpipe it will sever an artery in his neck. Either way he dies quickly. I'll attack from behind, with the quick sweeping slash I've practiced in front of every bathroom mirror in the Lodge. Killing him from behind, without seeing his face, bothered me a little. It seemed cowardly, but it was my only chance. The Ranger's manual also showed a counter move, a duck and sweep with the strong side elbow. So he does have a chance, at least. If he remembers that move, I will be the one with a knife in the neck.

I wipe the center of the mirror, watching the man emerge. Strong. Smart. True. I clean the mirror thoroughly from edge to edge. I can see myself and, looking back through the open doors behind me, the rest of my kingdom: the untidy bedroom, the Lodge itself.

Laughter drifts in from the hallway. Laughter and singing. Most guests are gone for the day, up on Tescher's mountain, tracking up the foot of new snow that fell in the night. I tuck the knife back into my shirt and stand alert, tilting my head to hear better. Singing. It's Stephanie's voice and some others. She's singing, but it's not her song.

"We're…off to see the wizard, the Wonderful Wizard of Oz…"

Stephanie laughing. The sound pierces my heart. She hasn't laughed for weeks, not since it became clear that Tescher would pass her over again for Olympic tryouts.

"…we hear he is a wiz of a wiz if ever a Wiz there was…"

I walk cautiously out into the room, listening. There are other voices too, men's voices, singing with her.

"…if ever oh ever a wiz there was…"

They're coming closer. I'm still holding my spray bottle stupidly in one hand as if it's some protection against whatever is coming.

"…the wiz is one because because…"

Two other voices. Two men. The hair stiffens on the back of my neck. One of the voices belongs to Bucky Price. Stephanie is *singing* with her father, the man she asked me to kill. And the other? What other strange voice falls on my ears, harsh as clattering garbage cans?

"…because because because because because…"

It is Nate Tescher. He hasn't set foot in the Lodge for as long as I've lived here. Now he is singing—singing!—with Stephanie and Bucky. What new madness is this?

"…because of the wonderful things he does!"

I step out into the hall. The three of them gallop toward me arm in arm, singing, giggling, stumbling. Price, on one end, was not the person I knew. Smiling and lighthearted, he'd been somehow transformed.

Tescher, the lumbering thug, was red faced and nearly delirious. Tiny Stephanie, squeezed between them, had also been released from some dark curse. I had never seen her so happy. The sight burned me inside.

They all saw me at the same time and stopped, still laughing. The three seemed so genuinely happy that for a moment I was drawn in. The edges of my mouth twitched, looking for an excuse to smile.

"Oh look," Stephanie said, "It's the maid."

Tescher guffawed, slapping the knees of his red snowsuit. Bucky Price dissolved his smile and closed his arms, drawing Stephanie closer to him. "Now hon," he said.

My head felt light. After a season of skiing the steepest terrain on loose-heeled Telemark gear, my balance was excellent. But here, flat footed on the plank floor of the Lodge, I was having trouble standing upright.

"I've got a job too, you know," Stephanie said. She threw her hands in the air and wiggled, an exotic celebratory dance. "I'm going to the Olympics."

"Now hon," Price said. "It's only the tryouts."

"I'm going." Stephanie closed her eyes and twirled slowly, snapping her fingers and repeating it over and over. "I'm going. I'm going."

"She's going all right, Bucky," Tescher said. "I've seen everyone else this year. Believe me there's no one like our girl."

He put one fat hand on her back. Raw bile rose in my throat. Stephanie stopped twirling, grabbed his hand and kissed it. "We're...OFF to see the wizard..."

They linked up again and continued down the hallway, pushing me aside. I work my jaw, trying to find the right position, the right expression to face the inconceivable. She's found another way. She's made some deal with them, something beyond my understanding, except that I was being tossed aside. Stephanie will go to the Olympics. I will be dropped into hell.

Their voices echo and rattle through the huge lodge, falling through the high log beams, circling into the vast open space between the log walls and the river stone fireplace, the granite hearth where the old Te-schers lie rotting. The song, the laughter, don't dissipate in that emptiness but instead swirl and gather, building echoes upon echoes until the whole Lodge, the whole Valley, is laughing, a deafening, harsh shriek of scorn and ridicule.

CHAPTER 30

Jason pulled on the handle of the metal basement door and then kicked as hard as he could. He kicked again and again.

"Please stop, Jason." Wallace Collins said. "You're making a great deal of noise."

"I can't believe that bastard just locked us in here," Jason said. "He's crazy. Everybody in this town is crazy."

"I was a fool to involve myself with these people," Collins said. "I don't believe that nonsense about a feud between Price and Tescher. I think Price is keeping us down here until Tescher can cash my check."

Darla crossed the room and looked at the steel door. "There's no way you're going to break that down, Jason," she said. "I wonder if we can pick the lock?"

Jason snorted. "Tell you what," he said. He nodded his head toward Kyle, who was still sitting on the small desk in the corner, idly pulling the drawers in and out with his toes. "If there was a big fatty on the other side of this door, we'd be out of here already."

Wallace Collins stood up from his chair, as if ready to take definitive action, but then winced and sat back down. "Damn my ankle," he said. He jammed a fist into an open hand. "I won't let myself be robbed by those devils."

Darla folded her arms and frowned. "Kyle," she said. "See if there's some sort of sharp metal object in that desk."

"Like what?"

"I don't know what. Something we can use to pick the lock."

Kyle, still using his feet, started pulling out the top drawer of the desk.

"Let's not fool around, Kyle." Wallace Collins said. "This is a serious situation."

The drawer tipped and then fell to the ground. Pencils and pens rolled across the concrete. Manila folders stuffed with papers and a stack of worn spiral bound notebooks slid across the floor.

"Kyle!"

"Shut up! You told me to look."

"Pick that all up right now," Darla said.

"You told me to look. I was looking."

"Pick it up."

"Fuck you," Kyle said, and turned to face the concrete block wall.

Darla bent over and picked through the papers littering the floor. "These belonged to Mr. Price's son," she said. "That poor boy who was killed in an avalanche. It's weird how no one ever mentions him."

Jason flipped through one of the spiral bound books, a blue one. "Poetry," he said, laughing. "Very, bad high school poetry. Listen." He struck a pose.

The night of storms has gone

The sunshine bright and clear...

Darla snatched it away. "At least he wrote *something*," she said. "If this was your notebook it would be full of drawings of naked women."

"Nude anatomical studies you mean."

"Shut up for a minute." She drew the notebook closer, squinting. She read aloud:

> *I am the only being whose doom*
> *No tongue would ask, no eye would mourn;*
> *I never caused a thought of gloom*
> *A smile of joy since I was born*
> *In secret pleasure, secret tears*
> *This changeful life has slipped away*
> *As friendless after fourteen years*
> *As lone as on my very first day*

"It's so *lonely*," Darla said. She turned the worn notebook over in her hands and then sat down and leafed through the pages.

"It's crap," Jason said.

"How would you know? What do you know about poetry, mister anatomical studies? There's some real power here." She whispered a few lines. These were voices from this alien world, cries of pain leaking out from the emptiness.

Kyle suddenly called out from the corner of the room. "Is *this* the dude?" he said.

Darla and Jason both turned. Kyle had taken another drawer out of the desk and was digging through it. He held a yellow newspaper clipping in his hand. Darla took it away. " 'Sunny Valley brothers sweep winter Karnival again' " she read. "There's Thad and I guess you're right, Kyle. This must be Andy, the other boy."

"I know that fuck," he said.

"How can you know him," Darla said. "He died in an avalanche." She squinted at the picture. "Look at those eyes. Here he's won some ski race but he doesn't look very happy. He just looks lost." She sighed. "Lonely and lost."

"His name ain't Andy," Kyle said. "He started work in the ski shop right before you guys got here. Tescher knows him. Lance and the Coyotes, they all know him."

There was a grunt behind them. Collins was on his feet. "Let me see," he said.

Darla walked two steps and handed him the fragile paper. Collins held it unsteadily in his fingers. "This is the boy who died?" he said. "Price's other son?"

"I guess," Darla said. "Who else could it be? I bet he had some of his own clippings up here but they've been taken away." She pointed to the blank space beside the desk marred with brown rectangles of old scotch tape.

"This is Price's boy?" Price asked insistently. "This is Andy?"

"I'm telling you his name ain't no fuckin' Andy," Kyle said. "I know that fuck. He ain't dead, but when I find that dude I'm going to cut his nuts off."

"Shut up, Kyle. What's wrong, Dad?"

Wallace Collins sank back down onto the cot, his mouth open. The newspaper clipping slipped between his fingers and onto the floor. "He's not dead," Collins said. "He killed Thad Price. Now he's going to kill us all. I sent that boy here from Presserton. He said he could convince Price to sell. I thought he would just push him around a little, perform a little vandalism. I had no idea he knew Price, that there was some connection between them." Collins covered his face in his hands. "Tescher said I'd opened the gates of hell and now I understand what he meant. We'll all be destroyed in the fire."

CHAPTER 31

Tescher kicked at the icy crust and rime at the granite step. He coughed and spat, kicking and kicking with his skis until he finally got a purchase. His hands were clammy with sweat inside his gloves. Another series of kicks and a burst of profanity and Tescher was up on the ridge.

He bent over, gasping for breath, and then dropped to his knees and vomited in the snow. Stephanie, that cold little bitch. What the hell was she doing sneaking up onto Little Spring Ridge just before Karnival? She was playing some game of her own now, he was sure of it. Somehow she'd found out that Andy was back. She was probably meeting him on the ridge to win him to her side. She would work her magic on him and screw the whole game. Tescher peeled off his gloves and wiped his eyes. He covered one nostril with a thumb and blew his nose into space. The magic wasn't going to work this time, though. Andy was free now and he was here for blood. He'd proved that already. Tescher covered the other nostril and blew again. Thad was just the start.

Dagger moon. Tescher's mother, Anna Tescher, had called the first quarter the dagger moon, so everyone else did too. "We'll live together under the dagger moon, Nate," she'd sing to Tescher when he was a little boy, stroking his hair. This was before Caroline was born, before Tescher understood how unimportant he was in this world. His mother had known all along, of course, but still she sang and sang.

The dagger moon, the Karnival moon, was high in the sky, embedded in the cloud of stars overhead. It gave little light but the star glow on the snow pack was enough. Sharp trunks of dead juniper trees, pale and shadowed, tilted at angles under the night glow. They looked like doomed marching soldiers. Tescher tried not to look at them but instead squinted

into the blue shadows of the snow, looking for tracks. Here were the deep
hollows of a deer caught on the ridge much too late in the season. Instead
of the neat cloven tracks that deer usually leave, there were gouges where
it struggled against the deep snows. He also saw tracks of two coyotes
walking unhurried, their paw prints in tidy lines. Tescher laughed. If he
were to follow the prints back along the ridge a few hundred feet he knew
he'd find the deer, stripped now to a skeleton, its skull cracked by powerful canine jaws and the brains licked out.

The image excited him. Tescher unzipped his snow suit and reached a
bare hand in to fondle himself, to get his juices flowing. Bucky Price and
his little witch Stephanie were full of shit. Caroline had been too, and Tescher's mother. He understood that now finally. Power wasn't a bunch of
stories and songs, Halloween nonsense that wouldn't scare a five year old.
Dig your teeth into someone's neck and rip. Fuck them while their blood
was still hot. Open their skull and lick out the brains. That was power.
Stephanie, Caroline, Anna—that whole line of witch-women and their
mates. They ruled Sunny Valley through ignorance. Protect us and you'll
thrive, they'd said. They lied. Now Tescher was going to break the spell.
Price had tried and failed, but Tescher would succeed. Fear and ignorance
would be gone. Hate would take its place.

Tescher saw a hint of tracks heading south, toward the point. There
was even a glow in that direction, a flickering yellow light. He spat again
and zipped himself up. Whatever she was doing, she was obviously ignorant to the fact that he had followed her, which was good. Tescher slid
along the ridge toward the yellow glow, trying to be quiet. Soon he could
hear her singing, that same tuneless, wordless song. Saliva rushed into Tescher's mouth. It was his sister's song, his mother's song, his grandmother's song. It was that old mystery bullshit. He spat.

At twenty or so paces away, Tescher ducked behind one of the thick
dead junipers and took off his skis. They were very near where Tescher's
sister Caroline was buried. Stephanie kneeled in the snow in front of a
small fire she'd built on a pine stump. She'd taken off her silver jacket
and wore only ski pants and a tight white thermal top that shimmered in
the starlight. She was lit by a yellow glow as she dug newspaper scraps
and strips of old cloth out of her pack and fed them into the fire. Her voice

rose and fell. Again, Tescher heard his mother, felt the long lovely fingers in his hair. "I'm the fourth," she said, touching his ears with her lips. "Your sister Caroline is the fifth. You have to protect us, Nate. Protect us always."

Tescher turned cold. Protect us. His mother had tortured him with those words from the day he was born. Protect your mother, protect your sister. Protect us, it's your duty. He did protect them and what did he end up with? Nothing. He was bankrupt. Less than nothing.

"Ah- a la la la. Ah- a la la la. Ah..."

The song surrounded him. It was all a fraud. He had no duty. The whole story had made him a coward. It would end now.

Tescher moved from behind the tree, making deep awkward steps in the snow. His breath came hard.

"Ah- a la la la. Ah- a la la la."

"Stephanie."

Stephanie stopped singing but didn't turn. The fire had grown larger, lighting her face and body with a beautiful glow. As Tescher watched she pulled a pair of old blue jeans out of her pack and placed them on the fire.

"Stephanie." Tescher tried to take another step forward but couldn't move. "What are you burning?" he said. Suddenly he could not catch his breath. "Burning isn't until tomorrow."

"I'm the sixth," Stephanie said. "I can burn whenever I want."

"Stephanie. All this crap is over. I've sold the mountain. Bucky *has* to sell. You'll never take possession. It's over."

"No it's not. You're here now. I'm burning. I'm going to bring him back and everything will be alright again."

"Bring who back?"

"Andy. He's near, I can feel it. I'm bringing him back and we're going to get married. We'll have a daughter, a cute little girl."

"You stupid cunt. He's already back. *I'm* the one who found him and brought him back to Sunny Valley. He's not going to marry you. He hates you. He already killed Thad. He's going to kill Bucky tomorrow and then he's going to kill you. He's going to slit your pretty white belly open and I'm going to watch."

"I'm bringing him back. He's mine. He always has been." She stood up and turned to face Tescher. Firelight glowed behind her, playing in the highlights of her hair so that she herself seemed to be on fire. She put her hands on her hips. "I'm the *sixth*, Mister Tescher. Sunny Valley is mine. It always will be."

Tescher lumbered forward and snatched Stephanie up as if she were a doll. One large gloved hand clamped around her throat while the other grabbed at her white thermal shirt, ripping. Stephanie flailed and kicked but his arms imprisoned her. She could do nothing against Tescher's bulk. He grunted. "You stupid...fucking...cunt." Tescher's free hand was on the waist of her ski pants now, pulling violently.

There was movement behind him, a swift shadow. It slid from the darkness near the Juniper trees and into the yellow light where Tescher and Stephanie struggled. Tescher jerked suddenly upright and then, very slowly, his knees bent. He lowered Stephanie onto the snow. His arms released her and she was able to scramble away. His right hand, which had been around her throat, now reached up to his own, touching delicately into his beard as if looking for something precious and lost. Blood poured over his fingers.

"Ah- a la la la. Ah- a la la la." Stephanie stood up and began to sing as Tescher crumpled onto the snow. She moved her hands over his body, found the pools of blood under his chin and smeared it over herself, face, hands, arms, belly and breasts. "Ah- a la la la. Ah- a la la la." Slowly she pulled the knife from Tescher's throat, feeling the warm blood cover her hands. She pricked her own finger with the tip of the knife and then held the knife out towards the moon, now almost completely settled on the ridge.

"You did it. You DID it!" she said. "You came back. You protected me, just like you were supposed to."

Stephanie zipped up her silver jacket and kicked back into her skis. She turned away from Tescher's body and faced the trunk of the dead juniper, now turning black as the moon went down. She spread her hands toward the starred sky above spoke:

> *Woods you need not frown on me*
> *Spectral trees that so doefully*
> *Shake your heads at the dreary me*

You need not mock so bitterly

"You can come out now," she said. "Come out and we'll get married. We can go to the Lodge and stand in the sacred spot. Where Granpa and Granma are buried. They'll marry us. I know they will."

The pale tree lost its remaining light and became a black hole on the ridge. Wind came up the slope, light at first and then stronger, carrying a solitary cold. Stephanie waited, standing ready on her skis, but no one emerged from the shadows.

CHAPTER 32

April used the tiny mirror on her lipstick case to adjust her hair band and big sunglasses. She and Candy had decided weeks ago that the look on the slopes for this Karnival thing should be pure sixties—Jackie O. and *entourage*. April wore skintight black pedal pushers and a Honey West-style clingy sweater. Candy had found a white-on-white snow bunny suit and was dragging around a ridiculous fuzzy muff made out of some dead animal.

It was all perfect except that no one was taking the least notice. There was harldy anyone at this pathetic resort anyway, but Candy and April had also spent good vodka money on private ski instructors and so far they were total duds, paying no attention to them whatsoever. It was like April and Candy were ghosts or something.

April twisted around in the lift chair and looked back at Candy who was in the chair behind. One good thing about this place was that the lifts were so slow you didn't have to waste a lot of time skiing. Candy's instructor was a seriously cute South American boy with long black eyelashes to die for, but he may as well have been back in beaner land. Candy's ski suit was unzipped to the waist and she'd practically wriggled out of it but Eyelash Boy seemed more interested in the tips of his skis.

April's guy, Lance, was even worse. He was tall and powerful-looking but he was *old*—over thirty, she guessed—and his skin looked like some kind of meat left in the sun to dry. He'd said four words to her so far, none of them using more than one syllable. April had tried out more than a few Honey West sweater moves just to see if he was alive, but he slumped disinterested on his half of the chair, smoking a cigarette.

Only one thing had stirred their interest so far. Right when the chairs started up the steep, *steep* part of the mountains, April saw Lance sit up. He leaned forward and looked intently at the icy rock face ahead of them. There-there! Something was moving quickly downward, barely touching the snow. Someone was actually skiing down that cliff! The Lance guy flexed his hands around his ski poles as he watched and his mouth fell open slightly.

The skier was a girl in a silvery jacket and shoulder-length blond hair that flew behind her in flash of light. She was short and compact and seemed to be incredibly light—her skis just touched the mountain in the few places where there was any snow at all. The rest of the time she seemed to be flying, arcing gracefully over the severe rocky face.

Lance leaned and turned to watch the girl finish her run down the mountain. Candy's guy, Mister Eyelashes, was watching too. So these guys *were* alive. You just had to do something dangerous get their attention.

A breeze rocked the chair lift slightly and when it passed through the rollers on the next tower the chair swung through a stomach-churning arc. April looked backwards to watch Candy's chair do the same thing at the tower. Candy screamed and grabbed Eyelashes. He jumped in such surprise that they both almost fell off the chair. Wouldn't *that* be romantic: Candy and her Latin stallion found dead in each other's arms among the beautiful snow-covered boulders below.

Poor girl. At least she was trying. April considered herself to be a person of privilege but she never wanted it said that she didn't at least try.

"What does *that* mean?" she said, poking a finger into her ski instructor's shoulder.

Lance lit another cigarette but said nothing.

"This patch on your jacket. Why do you have a patch with a dog on it? I think dogs are *so* cute."

"It's not a dog," he said. "It's a coyote."

" 'Flying Coyotes' Is that a clothing store?"

He twisted. The wooden slats of the seat under him complained. "No it's not a fucking clothing store." Got him! thought April. "It's Ski Patrol," he said. "That's the name of Sunny Valley Ski Patrol."

"That is so cool. *I* want to be a Flying Coyote. I would love to have a jacket like that."

Lance snorted. "You can't just join. Coyotes are the elite. We do all the rescue, all the avalanche. You gotta know what you're doing."

"It sounds *dangerous*."

"It is."

"You must be totally, like, buff. Skiing and working out all the time."

"That's right." Lance stared at the top of the mountain as if it would never arrive.

"So show me."

"Huh?

"Show me some muscle! Puhleeze. I love buff guys." She tugged on his jacket. "I'm going to be a royal bitch until you do."

"You're a royal bitch already."

"I'll get worse. Or I'll scream. I'll start screaming and waving my arms and everybody will look at us."

Lance said something inaudible and shrugged off his jacket, leaving him in a tight blue shirt. April bundled the jacket in her arms. "Oh my," she said. "A real Flying Coyote jacket. The elite. I am getting so hot."

"Okay? You've had your little power trip for the day? I swear there's something about women when they get in this valley…"

"Now the shirt."

"What?"

"The shirt. You are so *buff*."

Lance skinned off his shirt and made a brief shiver as his bare torso met the cold mountain air.

"You're not as muscle-y as I thought," April said.

"Shut up and…"

"Oooops!" April leaned forward and let Lance's shirt and jacket fall out of her arms. They fluttered down through the air like big ravens before landing on the steep icy face below.

"You bitch! You fucking bitch!" Lance practically jumped off the chair, as if he could somehow reach down to his clothes. He scrambled back up and grabbed April by the hair. "Why'd you do that, you stupid fucking bitch? I should fucking throw *you* off."

He shook her so violently that it seemed for a moment that he really would throw her off the chair. His sunglasses slipped off and hung around his bare neck by a strap. His deeply inset green eyes turned to purple as she watched. April swallowed hard. This was a little more attention than she's bargained for but if he was going to throw her off the chair they were both going. She would make sure of that.

Lance bent her back, his eyes, flaming with hatred, boring into her own. His calloused hand closed around her throat. April had no breath in her but she looked up toward the top of the mountain and then back at Lance. Again she looked up and then back. Finally Lance himself looked up the hill and saw that they were almost at the top, well in sight of the lift landing shack and a dozen or so skiers clustered around it.

He released her and sat back. April took a huge breath and, trying not to gasp too loudly, straightened her hair band and sunglasses.

"Stupid fucking bitch. I'm going to get reamed by the other guys. And now I gotta ski down there to get my jacket. I'm going to break my fucking neck and it'll be your fault."

"It was a total accident," April said. "Maybe that girl who was sking there before could pick it up for you."

"Shut the fuck up."

A few seconds passed in silence. They could see the lift shack clearly. The lift operator made obscene gestures through the window.

"I'm going to get reamed," Lance said.

"I said I was sorry. If there's anything I can do…"

Lance turned sideways and looked at April, as if for the first time. The rage was gone from his eyes and they had turned back to a distant, hollow green and black. He slipped the ski glove off his right hand and reached for her again. April flinched backward but his touch became gentle as he put his fingers to her face. "You coming to the Karnival parade tonight?" he said.

April nodded. His thumb moved over her cheeks, her lips. "You wanna be my date?" April nodded again, her skin tingling. His thumb found her mouth and pushed in. April touched it with her tongue and then nipped with her teeth. Lance jerked his hand back.

"Gotta go!" April said. They were at the lift shack. April jumped off the chair and skied away, leaving Lance staring back down the steep rocky face.

CHAPTER 33

Twenty one. Twenty two. She has left me.

Sweat curls around my ears and drips into my eyes, stinging. *Twenty three.* A pool forms on the floor. I touch it with my nose with each push-up. *Twenty four and five.* Sweat under my hands leaves a mark, however temporary, on the concrete floor. *Twenty six. Twenty seven.* She has left me.

Outside a record snowfall fills the night, fills the Valley. Seven feet are expected by morning. *Twenty eight.* With my mind I look into the dreams of the Lodge guests three floors over my head. I've washed and folded their sheets, made their beds, scraped their beer vomit from the carpets. Now I'm entitled to their dreams. Mine have been taken from me. Tonight they ski endless, weightless powder runs on wide open slopes. They turn with grace and form. They star in ski videos. Their minds are empty of the harsh reality of winter, of buried cars, frozen water pipes, timber roofs groaning under the weight, the terrible weight, of snow.

Twenty nine. She has left me. The air in my basement room is hot and acid dry. It crosses my throat and lungs without mercy, barely giving more than it takes, but I breathe steadily. *Thirty.* I'm used to it.

I lower down into my own sweat on the concrete floor and let the burning in my chest subside. I count again, this time to twenty. I count because that's as much rest as I allow myself. I count because counting is the only thing that empties my mind of everything, of hope and heartbreak, of rage and despair. Of Stephanie. Of murder. The numbers tick through my head. Sweat dribbles out of my body. Breath followed hot breath. She has left me. It is all without meaning.

I placed my hands for more pushups but before I can start there's a rap on the steel door. It could not be Bucky Price. He has a sharp, demanding knock, and anyway since our fist fight three weeks ago he hasn't come to the basement. It wasn't Stephanie; she's in Colorado Springs training with the Olympic team. She doesn't knock anyway but kicks at the door with the toe of her ski boot.

Not Stephanie nor Bucky. There were few other stars in my empty cosmos. The knock was light, rhythmic, in the pattern of "shave and a haircut". I stood up, wiped my hands, and walked quickly to open the door. It was Thad, back from Europe.

"It's about time, Assface," he said, knocking the snow from his jeans and shirt. It's late and the night is dim with the thick curtain of falling snow but he's wearing sunglasses, a cheap mirrored pair with white plastic frames. "It's really pounding out here," he said. "I practically had to swim across the parking lot."

I haven't seen him since Christmas. He's taller and thinner, with jaw and cheekbones now clearly defined into deep, handsome lines. A small lump formed in my throat. I tried to swallow, to breathe. I want to look into his eyes, but he's still smiling at me from behind sunglasses. I see only myself.

"Assface." Thad held out his hand. Just as I took it he swung his left in a big round house punch that would have caught me on the side of the head if I hadn't been ready for it. I grabbed his hand in mid air and twisted, spinning him around and forcing his arm up behind his back.

"You're pretty quick now, Assface," Thad said, laughing.

"You never were."

"Okay, you win. I'm worn up, washed out. The freakin' ladies on the tour are killin' me."

I let go. Thad shook his arm out but didn't turn back to face me. Instead he paced around my basement room. He wiped his forehead with his shirt. "It's like hell down here, Assface. How can you stand it?"

"I'm used to it."

"Tell dad to give you a real room upstairs. One with some air."

I said nothing.

Thad walked to the far wall, to my collection of newspaper clippings. He ignored Stephanie's and focused on the others: his victories and a few of my own. The latest were glossy and in color, photos from European ski magazines showing Thad in action on his current freestyle tour, sponsored by a rich ski manufacturer.

"You've got it all here, Assface. How 'bout this 180 fakie invert? That was in Basel. You do something like that on the tour and the chicks squeal like little pigs."

"What happened? Why are you back?"

Thad waved a hand over his shoulder. "Six day break. Thought I'd come back and revisit my roots. How's that Assface? You're one of my roots. Make sure you tell that to the Warren Miller crew when they're here in the spring."

Something was wrong. Thad was being Thad but there was an edge to his voice, a shrillness I'd never heard before. Was it true that this was just a break in the tour? Or had something happened in Europe to bring him back? I couldn't imagine what would scratch at his confidence, his usual bold mastery of the world.

"When did you get here?" It was all I could think of to say.

"Three lovely hours ago. Right when the storm was really sinking in. The highway's closed above Pine Butte but I got my Scout out of Alex's garage and drove on up. Had to go fast to keep from getting stuck. It was like riding a giant Ski-doo."

Something *was* wrong. Thad and I had stayed friends through high school but he was closest to his ski patrol buddies, the Flying Coyotes. Last time he was home he spent his first few days drinking and laughing it up in the bunkhouse at the Ski Center. It wasn't until he was nearly ready to leave that he looked for me upstairs and spent a few hours telling me about the tour while I scrubbed and mopped. But now here he was only home for a few hours, pacing nervously in my room.

He was at the Stephanie wall now. Thad peeled a clipping off and held it with the tips of his fingers. "Want me to take these down for you, Assface?"

"Leave my stuff alone."

"She got there," he said, quietly. He carefully pressed the clipping back onto the wall. "She wanted to be on a cereal box. I hope it was worth it."

"Thad…"

He turned and took off the sunglasses. His face was drained of color—it was nearly blue under the fluorescent lights. Sweat covered his forehead. "I can't stand it here," he said. "Let's go upstairs and talk."

"I can't go up there. You know that."

"Dad's gone. He's over drinking with his new best friend, Nate Tescher. They're figuring out what to do with all the money they're going to make after they turn Sunny Valley into Disneyland on ice. With this snow he won't be back tonight."

"Thad…"

"C'mon. We'll sit in the bar upstairs. Like real people."

The Lodge was silent inside. The guests were in bed and the thick layer of fresh snow falling outside muffled what few sounds might creep in from the night. Thad and I crossed the open lobby, which was black except for a pool of lamplight at the front desk where Carlie snored in her chair. On the far side of the room Thad found by touch the knotted pine door of the bar and unlocked it with a key from his pocket. We went inside.

He flicked a single light and went behind the old bar. "Being eldest son carries a few privileges, at least," he said, digging among the bottles. "I may as well enjoy them while I can. What'll you have Assface?"

"Water."

Thad snorted. "I forgot you don't drink. Dad's put up some fancy Scotch back here. The rich flatlanders love paying ten bucks a glass for it. Sure you don't want to give it a try?"

"No."

Thad poured a glass for me and then nearly filled a brandy snifter with Scotch for himself. He sat on the barstool next to me. "Cheers," he said. I drank from my glass but Thad only dipped a finger in his Scotch and began to draw something on the counter top. I couldn't see what.

"What are you doing tomorrow?" he said.

"What do you think I'm doing?"

"Yeah, yeah, I mean besides that. You wanna ski? You wanna ski first thing? It's going to be pretty epic. Folks in Europe pay three or four hundred bucks to ski a few runs with Thad Price. You can go for free."

"What about the Coyotes?" I said.

"What about them?"

"I thought you'd want to go out with them early. Blast the avalanche chutes and overhangs."

Thad gulped his drink, draining almost half the glass. He screwed up his face and shivered. "Nah," he said. "Not those morons. Plus who wants to get up that early?"

"You used to like blasting."

"Look, shut up. Okay, Assface? Don't tell me what I like and don't like. Do you want to ski tomorrow or not? Don't worry about dad and the rooms and whatnot. Fuck Bucky. I'll take care of him."

"Yes."

Thad took the glass for another gulp but then thought twice about it. Again he wet his finger with Scotch and drew on the bar top. "I thought we might hit the ridge," he said, his voice quiet. "Mid morning."

"Hit where?"

"The ridge. Little Spring Ridge. Climb that baby. Ski the far chute. Should be epic."

I laughed and drank some water. "Right."

"No, I'm serious."

"Yeah. With all this new snow? Especially when the sun hits it? It's not going to be ski-able for a couple of days at the soonest."

Thad drew on the countertop again. His voice had shrunk to almost nothing and he himself seemed to be shrinking too. Suddenly we were eight year olds again, eating hot dogs at this same bar, kicking each other with our ski boots.

"You afraid?" he whispered. "I'm skiing at a whole different level now, Andy. I'd understand if you didn't want to go."

The room turned quiet again, so quiet I could hear the bubbles rise in my water glass. Thad had called me by my real name, something he hadn't done since we were kids.

Suddenly a voice interrupted: "Hey. Hey!" We both looked toward the door. A guest appeared, a red-faced man in boxer shorts and a tee shirt. A ridiculous knit cap perched on his head.

"This where the party's at?" he said.

"The bar's closed," Thad said. "Go back to bed."

"How 'bout a nite cap?" he said, pulling the hat off his head. "Get it? A night cap?"

Thad grabbed a ketchup bottle from behind the bar and flung it. It hit the door jamb and smashed, dripping red down the wall. "Get your butt out of here," Thad said. The man disappeared.

Thad again drew on the bar top. At some point he'd taken another huge slug out of his glass—it was barely a fourth full now. Did he really want to ski the ridge tomorrow? He must be drunk. It would be suicide.

Thad took a deep, deep breath. "Did you ever wonder what you're doing here?" he said.

"It was your idea," I said. The drink was clearly hitting him now. Thad's handsome face was nearly pressed down onto the bar.

"No, Andy. I mean *here*." A trickle of electricity awoke in my spine. I leaned close, wanting to hear him clearly. "Sunny Valley," he said. "Did you ever wonder what in the hell a kid like you is doing *here*?"

CHAPTER 34

There was a scrambling noise outside. The metal door opened and sunlight poured in. Darla was asleep at the foot of the steps. The light woke her. She looked up and saw the outline of someone standing in the doorway, a tall man surrounded by light.

"Mr. Price?" she said. The outline turned in the doorway and walked out of sight. Something stirred in her. It was a familiar shape but it was not Bucky Price.

"Wait!" Darla ran up the stairs and outside into the sunshine. He was walking away, down the recently shoveled path. Darla could see faded jeans and a worn blue jacket. "Stop!" she said. When he did not stop she ran a few more feet toward him. "I know who you are."

The man turned slowly. Her heart nearly stopped. It was the man she'd seen at the front desk their first night in Sunny Valley, the young Clint Eastwood. His hair was short and bleached by the sun, his face deeply tanned but also covered with freckles. He cocked his head to one side.

"You know who I em?" he said. "I wish I did. Tell me, then. Who em I?"

"You're *Andy*. Mr. Price's stepson. You lived down in that awful basement room. And you were killed in an avalanche! Why does everyone say you were killed in an avalanche?"

"Because I'm dead."

"You *are* him." Darla reached up and touched the side of his face. He blinked, but didn't move. "I've been wondering if I imagined it all. I read some of your poetry," she said. "It's so sad. This whole Valley seems closed in on itself."

"It's crep. It'll burn like everything else. I'm going to burn this place down," he said, putting one hand on the rough log exterior of the Lodge. "Collins and his sons will burn too if you don't get them up out of that hole. Not that I care."

Darla's hand went to her mouth. "And you were Stephanie's fiancé. That just clicked. You're the one she told me about. My god, Andy, does she know you're here? Does she know you're still alive?"

Andy said nothing. His jaw was tight.

"She's *obsessed* with you. She still thinks you're going to get married even though you're dead. I mean, I really think that accident must have drove her a little crazy. Oh my god, when she sees you…"

"She won't see me. She won't see it coming. That's only fair."

"I don't understand."

"You will. You will understand soon."

Darla was breathless. "You're going to kill her? Why? She *loves* you." The Andy that Darla had imagined down in the basement room was lonely, heartbroken. This Andy *was* that Andy, but there was something more. "What happened?" Darla said, trying to keep him from walking away. "You two were so much in love."

"I told you I was dead," he said. "She's the one who killed me. Why shouldn't she pay for it? It's what's fair."

"You're *not* dead. Why do you say that? Why does everyone say you died in that avalanche?"

"The rescue team didn't find me. They found Thad and took him out with the helicopter. Then they stopped looking. I was a hundred feet away under loose snow, not even buried."

"Didn't you call out to them?"

"I told you. I was already dead. She killed me. I was near paralyzed anyways. It came better later when I was in Texas."

"You went all the way to Texas after the avalanche? Why? Why when Stephanie was here *grieving* for you?" Darla thought she saw a glimmer of life in Andy's cold mouth. A touch of doubt, of surrender. "Why do you say *she* killed you? Didn't the avalanche kill you? I mean, I know you're not dead, but…"

"Darla!" Wallace Collins's voice came from behind her. "Darla, get away from him. That man is a murderer. He's the devil."

Andy's eyes made on last deep bore into Darla's and then he wordlessly turned away. He took a pair of lightweight skis from behind a propane tank and began to strap them on. "You'd better get your boys out quick, Collins," he said. "Or they'll be cooked."

"No, no," Collins said. "Our arrangement is terminated. I no longer have need of your services. I'm going to get my check back from Tescher and then we're leaving this place forever."

Andy made a narrow half smile. The sight turned Darla's legs to rubber. "It's terminated all right," he said. He stood up and strapped a pair of ski poles to his wrists.

Kyle and Jason stumbled into the light. Kyle collapsed onto his knees, holding his head in his hands. He looked around and saw Andy.

"You fuck," he said, shaking his head as if to clear it. He shook back his raggy, curly hair and pointed. "I'm going to kick your ass, you fuck."

"Come and get me," Andy said. "I'll give you a fair fight."

Before anyone could react, Kyle was on his feet, scrambling through the snow. Andy turned, pushed with his poles, and glided off through the meadow, kicking himself forward seemingly without effort.

"Kyle!" Wallace Collins shouted. "Come back here."

Kyle ran awkwardly through the knee-deep snow. After twenty yards he stopped, gasping. Andy glided around the corner of the Lodge and disappeared from view. Kyle caught his breath and ran again, kicking up snow.

"Kyle! Go get him, Jason."

"Um, Mr. Collins, I'm not sure that's a good idea."

"Jason!"

"Dad, *please*," Darla said. Clearly Andy had been transfigured by what had happened to him: changed physically and psychologically. But she couldn't believe he was a murderer, that the deep passion he'd once had was so far gone. "Kyle's not going to get very far in this snow, Dad. There's no way that Andy guy is going to waste his time. Kyle'll be back in a few minutes. Let's just figure out how we're going to get out of this place."

They followed the shoveled walkway around the building, toward the

Lodge parking lot, Collins limping painfully.

"Our car's burnt, Darla."

"I know that, Dad." She sighed. The Karnival was supposed to start this morning. Maybe there were actually some people here. "I'll find someone going down to Pine Butte and we can get a ride from them."

They turned the corner and faced the parking lot. The burnt rental car was gone, as was any sign of last night's bonfire. Instead the parking lot was freshly plowed and full of people in colorful ski clothes. Pavillion tents served hot chocolate and Polish sausages. A platform stood in the center where a dozen children participated in a snowman building contest.

Stephanie Price, smiling and laughing, helped the children pack snow into chubby shapes. On her head was a small wreath of green pine boughs. Bucky Price walked among the children. He wore a fur hat and coat and held a wooden staff streaming with ribbons. Wallace Collins, Darla, and Jason watched open-mouthed as Price put a rhinestone star on one of the snowmen and then reached down to receive a tremendous hug from the fat red-faced child who had built it.

CHAPTER 35

The dark air of the Lodge bar held no oxygen.

What was I doing here? It was the question I'd asked myself since birth. It was the question I'd asked of Bucky, Thad and Stephanie. I'd asked it of the deep snow and harsh light of Sunny Valley. It was the question that defined me when nothing else could. Now Thad, well into nearly a half bottle of scotch, was asking me if I wanted to know the answer.

During my second season in Sunny Valley one of Thad's ski team buddies sucker punched me while we were getting off a lift together, catching me in the gut just as my skis hit snow. I fell, splay legged, looking like I had never dismounted a chair lift before. The junior ski team and the coach--Nate Tescher--stood around and laughed while I tried to get my breath and climb back to my feet. Thad, riding the chair behind me, must have seen what happened, but he said nothing. He never explained to them that I was not who they thought I was, that the world was just unfair. Why now? Was he finally going to stand up for me?

"Thad, you don't need to tell me anything."

"Shut up, Assface. Just hang on."

Thad stood and leaned over the bar. I thought he was going to be sick but he was just digging around on a shelf.

"Freak," he said. "Where is it?"

"What..."

"Just shut up a minute." Thad walked all the way around and ducked down. Everything was quiet for a moment and I was alone in the gloom. I sincerely wondered if I was in a dream. The flatlanders snoring in the rooms around us dreamed of skiing endless powder. I dreamed of learning who I was.

Thad burped loudly and there was a smashing of glassware. "Here," he said, slapping something on the bar top. "Read this."

On the scarred black bar lay a book, covered with dust. The page edges were browned and rough. I picked it up and read the spine. "Letters of the Gold Rush. Pine Butte Historical Society." I slumped on my bar stool. "What does this have to do with me?"

"Just read it," he said. "There should be a book mark at the right place. Right in the middle."

I opened the book and flipped the pages, looking for a bookmark. The pages were brittle and some shattered in my hand.

"Hey, be careful," Thad said. "That belonged to my mom."

The book had an old smell, a familiar smell. I held it close and sniffed. Rats. It smelled like the rat's nest I cleared out of the eaves last year. "Thad, what…"

"Just read it, Andy. Please. I'm not kidding. I know it's important to you. I'm not kidding."

Andy. He called me Andy. I found the bookmark and opened the page. I started at the top and read:

> *A letter from Hiram Dwight Pierce to his wife Amanda Pierce*
> *Dated March 10, 1850*
> *My Dear Amanda,*
> *I write in haste for we ride to Nevada City in two hours time. There are trappers here who will take our letters to Carson and, thus, quickly to you. All in our party are writing like men possessed, even those with little in the way of literary art.*
> *I ask you, my darling, to take this letter to Mr. White to convey to the Territorial Governor as soon as possible. I hope my letter reaches him first, before the false and lying reports that are certain to follow. I am determined that my name be free of stain in this matter, that the true record of events be made clear.*
> *I must tell my story quickly.*
> *You and the Lord both know I accepted employment with the Surveyor General with the best intentions;-a sensible railroad passage through the Sierra will bring the benefits of civilization to Christian and heathen alike. Our party was assigned to the Border Ruffian Pass*

area, directly east of the Calaveras mining camps. Few white men have followed the Stanislaus River up into the high Sierra and those only trappers, not surveyors. We asked in the mining camps but there was little information as to the suitability of the route for passage of steam locomotives. These men care for blood and gold and nothing else.

I won't trouble you with our travails reaching the pass. Let me only say that God created no route less suitable for modern transportation. Steep granite outcroppings alternate with choked lodgepole forests. Our horses served only to carry our equipment since the country was too broken and dense for riding.

I'll remind you of the members of our party. In addition to Captain O'Shaunassy, representing the Surveyor General, was myself as assistant surveyor and Callahan, the wrangler. While provisioning in Calaveras the Captain hired a young man as cook. He'd found the boy outside our camp near starving. The boy said his family had been robbed of their gold claim and his parents killed. He had no money to return to relatives in Philadelphia and needed employment, however menial or dangerous. I heard a different story the next day at the Assay Office – that the young man himself had tried to jump a claim down on the Kern and killed two miners and their wives before being run off. I thought this was nonsense at the time, a tale to give us city folk a scare, so I did not repeat it to the captain. Oh, if I had, might the hand of God been moved?

After four days of difficult progress we could see that at last we were nearing the pass. That morning, as we rode into the rising sun, the thick lodgepoles cleared and we found ourselves at the entry to a pretty open valley, green with meadow grass...

"That's here," Thad said. "Sunny Valley."

"I figured as much." I said. I was still confused. Was I really going to learn something about myself? I looked at the clock behind the bar: almost 4am. In a few hours I would have to get started with my daily cleaning. Skiing was out of the question. Thad's challenge to ski Little Spring Ridge was just bluster.

"Keep reading," he said. "You need to know what it's all about."

"Okay, okay."

...The valley faced south and was filled with sunshine. The east rim was an elegant volcanic ridge and, behind, to the north, a good sized peak that would hold much game...

"That's the ski mountain now," Thad said.
"I get it. Do you want me to read or what?"
"Sorry."

...The valley floor was hazy with smoke and we were little surprised to find a settlement of Washoe encamped there. The Washoe live along the Sierra foothills but many families follow the game into the High Sierra in spring and summer.

The Captain ordered our horses released to graze. Callahan was instructed to pitch camp at the valley opening. I volunteered to take my rifle into the hills in search of game but the Captain observed that the Washoe would have cleared the hills of deer by now. In fact the Washoe men were probably away for some days, hunting high on the pass. Instead our young man, Tescher was his name...

I put the book down. "Not…"
"Yes. Keep reading."

...was told to approach the Washoe women and barter for meat and acorn mash.

I consider myself a good judge of character, but I must tell you Amanda that in our four days together I learned nothing of this young man. He spoke little. He was not hostile to me but neither was he friendly. The sole observation I had made was that he rarely slept. He sat up nights with his rifle cradled in his lap, staring into our camp-fire. He had the deep blue eyes typical of his Slavic forebears and in the firelight, where he stared unblinking for hours I thought sometimes I saw an unearthly glow. I wondered if he burned with pain over his lost family. I also thought again of the story I'd heard in Calaveras.

And so the boy Tescher crossed the valley to the Washoe camp. We were set about our various chores when a rifle shot was heard, then another and another. The Captain, Callahan and myself sprang up and ran toward the village as fast as we could, certain that Tescher had been ambushed by some Washoe men who had stayed behind in the camp. More shots were heard as we ran across the meadow—first three, then four, then four more. I thought that Tescher had taken a defensive position and was holding out desperately against the Washoe.

My imaginings were far from the truth. We entered the encampment cautiously but Tescher stood in the center, near the Washoe fire-pit, calmly reloading his rifle. Near his feet were four bodies-an old man with thick platted grey hair, a Washoe woman and two children. I stopped and stared, utterly shocked.

The Captain confronted Tescher, asking him the meaning of what we saw. Tescher was calm but I saw the fire of hell in his eyes. "My valley," he said. "This is my valley now."

I was frozen with horror, but Callahan walked among the huts, pulling open the hide doors to look inside. "He got 'em all," were his words. "Kids, women, old folks. I count twenty dead."

"Is this for real?" I said, but I knew it must be true. I could imagine every detail as if I had lived it myself.

"Mom thought so," Thad said. "Dad too. Mom said that it happened right here, where the old cabin used to be. Right where the Lodge is now."

"How did she know?"

Thad pressed his face to the bar again and closed his eyes. "She knew everything," he said. "She knew the past and the future. Keep reading."

Twenty! It was the slaughter of the innocents enacted before my eyes. I had heard stories of violence toward the Indians but never imagined I would see such things myself or participate in them.

The Captain swung the butt of his rifle and caught Tescher on the face. The boy went down but remained defiant. "This is my valley now," he said. "You'd best move on."

"If this be your land, you're welcome to it," the Captain said. "Come winter the snow here will be over your head. But the Washoe men will be back here before that. They won't take kindly to what you done. And you won't be able to shoot them in their beds."

The Captain and Callahan prepared to return to our camp but I protested. These people are heathen but they deserve a humane burial. I could not endure the idea of their bodies left outside for the vultures and coyotes to feast upon. The Captain allowed that there was no time, that we should press on for Border Ruffian Pass before the Washoe men returned. "We'll burn 'em," he said. "That should be good enough."

I cut brush for the pyre, sickened by my own action. Callahan and Tescher carried the bodies to the center of the camp and laid them on the mound of dry lodgepole and Manzanita I had built.

We stood back as the Captain lit the fire. I turned away entirely, unable to watch the horrid spectacle. The flames crackled and grew. It was the only sound I could hear besides Tescher's awful chuckling.

My dear Amanda, what I write next will sound utterly fantastic to you but I swear it is true. With the fire's heat on my back I could see the faces of Tescher and Callahan, both red from the flames. But as I watched both men became agitated. They yelled something I could not understand and ran forward, toward the fire. I couldn't imagine what would draw their attention so besides a wild animal or something equally dangerous. I turned and looked into the fire.

Amanda, though I pray every day for salvation I know now that I have seen the very fires of hell. Blackened bodies, seared of clothing, swelled and burst in the flames. A child's hand near to me moved in the heat, slowly closing, as if to pick up a toy. The faces of those innocents turned before my eyes into hollow blazing skulls, their jaws locked open in a perpetual scream.

But the other men were not watching the pyre. They saw, as I also saw, a silver shape in the flames, a figure, a girl! A young Indian girl walked toward us straight from the flames of the pyre. Her deerskin robe was in places singed and her face was smudged with ash but she seemed in no other way injured. She had evidently not died in Tescher's assault, indeed had not been shot at all, but had perhaps swooned, remaining unconscious until the fire woke her.

We all stood in dumb admiration as the girl approached Tescher. She somehow knew it was he who had perpetrated the massacre on her tribe, but she raised no cry. She knelt at his feet and folded her arms.

Darling Amanda, the trappers are at my tent flap saying they must be off. I'll quickly bring my testimony to a close and beg that you believe me, that every word is true.

The Captain, Callahan and I left immediately. Tescher made us to understand that he would take the Indian girl as his wife and that she had proposed to help him evade and defeat the Washoe when they returned, as long as she herself was protected.

We cared not for his safety or his prospects. We left Tescher in the strange hell he had created and hurried to Border Ruffian pass, anxious to put the stink of the funeral pyre far behind.

I must go. I forever remain,

Your loving Husband,

Hiram

I closed the book. Thad took it from my hands and put it to his face. He was crying.

"Now tell me," I said. "You said your mother knew everything. She told you. Now tell me."

"That was Cor Tescher," Thad said. "Nate Tescher says Cor was his great great grandfather."

"So that's how he got the mountain?"

Thad snorted. "Tescher doesn't own the mountain. He leases it from us."

"How did your dad get it then? What happened to the Tescher in the letter?"

"That Indian girl was called Little Spring. She helped Cor Tescher kill the Washoe men when they got back. She taught him how to survive through the winter. In exchange she made him promise that she would always be protected and that all her female children would be protected. Cor left the land not to his son, Dale, but to his *daughter*, Ann. My great great grandmother. *She* left it to her daughter Sophie. That's the deal: Sunny Valley always was passed on to the daughter."

"So Bucky married into it. Your mom actually held the deed."

"Yeah. He acts like he's king but he's just caretaker. Stephanie will own it when she turns twenty one."

"Does she know that?"

"Stephanie? Oh yeah. She knows this whole story better than I do. Who begat whom and all that. All I know is that mom's dad was a Tescher, someone from that old family who thought he could marry back in and get hold of the valley. Mom told me she didn't care at first. When she was a little girl she actually told her brother that he could have it. But it never happened. She married dad instead and had us. Had Stephanie, which is what really matters."

"And..."

Thad seemed entirely sober now. He was even cheerful, as if happy to finally tell the story to someone outside the tribal circle. "Mom had it rough. She didn't want the Lodge, the Ski Center, none of it. It was all Bucky. I think in the end mom didn't trust him. So they adopted you, a total outsider. She got you for Stephanie."

"I was adopted to be Stephanie's husband? When I was a little boy? You're crazy. "

"Well, as her protector anyway. But yeah, I think so. Mom used to joke about it, which would get dad really mad."

I was tumbling head first down a black diamond run. I was collapsed under a ski lift, sucker punched, gasping for air. I was on a chin-up bar with my fingers turning blue, trying to keep my bare feet out of the snow. I was standing in front of a closet mirror in one of the upstairs rooms, arm in arm with Stephanie, who had a toilet paper veil over her face. We were pretending to get married.

"But your mother died. I mean, I hardly remember her at all."

"That's why she wanted a protector. Mom knew she wouldn't be around when Steph turned 21. She made Dad promise, though. Promise to honor the tradition. She knew both him and Mr. Tescher wanted to take over the valley." Thad sipped from his drink. "Dad kept his promise. He was afraid not to."

"Afraid? Your dad?"

Thad rubbed his forehead with the palm of his hand. "It's hard to explain," he said. "You weren't born here, so..."

"So what?"

"Well, anyway, there was no way he was going to let you two get married. He wants to do what Tescher never could: stop that matrilineal thing."

"If Stephanie never marries, never has a daughter…"

"That's the idea."

"Well he doesn't have to worry about me, anyway. She hates me. She's gone to Colorado."

"That was the deal he cut with Tescher and Stephanie. It was pretty genius. Tescher would let her go to the tryouts if she stopped seeing you. In exchange Stephanie would sign over the Valley to Bucky and he would sell—really sell—the mountain to Tescher. Stephanie was so sure she was going to win a gold medal that she didn't care about any of the rest of it. The history and stuff."

"It worked."

"It didn't work. Steph isn't doing as well in Colorado as everyone thought she would. It's like she goes out of the valley and all her magic powers go away or something. She might get cut from the team any day now and come back here."

I put my hands to my forehead. It was burning hot. Stephanie was coming back to Sunny Valley. Stephanie who I was destined to love and protect. Stephanie who tore my heart out with her own two small hands.

"She's coming back," I said. "The deal is off. She could marry, have a daughter. So now you have to…"

"I don't have any choice, Andy. You know that. Bucky called my in Zurich. Said I had to come back here."

"So that's why you want to ski the ridge tomorrow? Right after a big snowfall? It's not just for old time's sake."

Thad was drunk again. He was loose, uncontrolled, sloppy. He put his head down on the bar. Saliva poured out of his mouth. He fumbled at his shirt and ripped it off, as if he was in unbearable heat. "I just want to ski," he said. He choked down a sob. "I want to ski with you."

"You want to kill me," I said.

CHAPTER 36

"Good news for you, Mr. Collins," Stephanie said. "This is the best turnout for Karnival in years. The mountain is so busy!"

Wallace Collins, looking pale and drained, limped forward. One hand gripped Jason's shoulder, the other held the collar of his ski jacket closed, as if he were standing in an icy wind instead of Sierra sunshine. He strained forward, trying to look over the heads of the people surrounding the stage where the snowman contest was now breaking up. "Where is your father, Stephanie?" he said. "I saw him a moment ago. I must speak to him."

Stephanie smiled with sweet benevolence. "I imagine he took the Ski-doo up to the mountain. The races need setting up and Daddy usually helps." Stephanie turned her dazzling smile toward Jason. "What about you?" she said. "Did you register for the Doofus race?"

"The what?"

"It's a race for flatlanders. We do it every year. It's just for people who've never raced before."

"Uh, no, I didn't register. And actually I have raced a few times."

"That's okay," Stephanie said, still smiling. "You can still be in the Doofus race. Tell the starters I said it was okay."

"Gee thanks."

Stephanie turned toward Darla. "Why don't we take a few runs to-gether?" Stephanie's face radiated happiness. "It's such a *beautiful* day."

Darla bit her lip. It *was* a beautiful day, with all the sunshine and blue skies the Sierras were famous for. The children at the winter Karnival had linked hands in a big circle and were now singing and kicking their feet up like chorus girls, filling the snowy parking lot with noise and laughter. A group of teenagers standing near the hot cocoa tent applauded. It all looked so normal, so perfect. Suddenly the events of the night and day before seemed unreal. Had their car really been burned in the parking lot? Had they been locked all night in the cellar room of a lonely forgotten boy who had died tragically in an avalanche? And had that boy, now twisted with hatred, come to life the next morning to rescue them? Only moments ago, Darla had had so much to tell Stephanie, but now none of it seemed to make sense.

Wallace Collins shook his head, his mouth gripped tight. "I have no time for this," he said. "Let's get up to the mountain, Jason. We will get my check back from Tescher and Price. And I'm sure we will find Kyle. Perhaps he has already gone up to confront them on my behalf."

"Do you know where to board the shuttle bus?" Stephanie said, helpfully.

Jason looked up at the mountain and blinked. He'd left his sunglasses in the basement room and now everything hurt his eyes. "Mr. Collins," he said, "I gotta think we'd be better off if we just got down the hill. Head on down to Pine Butte. Maybe later we can…"

"I'm going," Collins said. "I won't let those men bankrupt me and humiliate my son. I will go myself if you won't take me."

Jason looked around at Darla, who just shrugged and held up her hands. Jason frowned and then started to lead Collins across the parking lot. After a few steps he turned. "Shouldn't you stay with us, Squeaker?" he said. "I mean, are you really going skiing?"

"Oh yes," Stephanie replied. "Darla *loves* to ski."

Their lift ride up was a complete failure. Stephanie chatted steadily about ski wax, snow conditions, and a new kind of ski boot she'd seen someone wearing. Darla sat on her half of the creaking chair, opening and closing her mouth like a fish, trying to get a word in edgewise. That Andy guy is *not dead*, she wanted to say. He's come back to Sunny Valley, but he's *changed*. He's not the boy you loved, who helped to break your loneliness. His own loneliness has taken him over like a cancer.

But not a syllable of this got out before they reached the lift house and Stephanie slid away toward the upper bowl. Darla trailed behind, flailing her skis and poles to try to catch up.

"Right over here, Darla," Stephanie called out. Was she *trying* to avoid talking about Andy, about what had happened last night? Did she already know? Or was she just weird old Stephanie, skiing away in her own little world?

Darla stopped a few feet from the edge of the bowl. She inched her skis closer to the edge and craned her neck to look down. She could see nothing at first, only emptiness. Leaning a little more she could finally see the actual run, a seemingly vertical white face bordered on both sides by craggy rocks. The slope was cut abruptly at the bottom by a stand of pine trees. "Stephanie," she said, "I'm not sure I can do this. It's pretty steep."

"Sure you can. Remember to lift, just like I showed you. Lift right up out of your boots. Don't *try* to turn, let the mountain turn for you. Close your eyes if you want."

"It's just that…"

It was too late. With barely a whisper of skis on snow, Stephanie disappeared over the cornice. Darla saw the flash of Stephanie's silver jacket as she made a few fast turns and then twirled to a stop at the tree line.

Darla backed away from the edge, took off her gloves and wiped her face with her hands. Darla *loves* to ski, Stephanie had said. Maybe so, maybe this week of skiing the Valley with Stephanie's really had helped. But at the moment loves-to-ski Darla had an enormous knot of fear in her throat. She was going to have to ski down what looked like one of the steeper sections of Mt. Everest without killing herself. Again Darla edged her skis to the rim. Stephanie was standing just at the trees now, waving her poles.

Darla loves to ski. Okay. Darla swallowed hard and gripped her poles. "Lift out of your boots," Stephanie had said. Oh, she'd lift all right.

Darla bent her knees deeply and threw herself off the rim. Her skis, her legs, her whole body disappeared from under her and she became weightless, nothing but cold air and adrenaline. She'd thrown herself so far forward that she seemed to be flying--superhero-style-- down the mountain.

Darla's skis touched. She bent her knees, feeling her stomach in her boots. At that moment Stephanie, standing at the trees, threw her hands in the air. Darla did the same, leaping high, leaping out of the turn and into another superwoman launch down the mountain.

She made only one more turn, one more brief touch of skis on snow, one more leap into the void, before the slope flattened out in front of the trees. Darla, breathing like she'd run a hundred miles, made three quick regular turns to control her speed but she was still going too fast. Finally she lay back and let her skis run in front of her. She dug her elbows into the snow, sliding to a stop right at Stephanie's feet.

Darla shrieked. "Oh…my…GOD!"

"You took that just right," Stephanie said, beaming. "See what I mean by lifting out of your boots?"

"Oh god," Darla stood up and brushed herself off. She looked back up the slope. "I can't believe I really skied that. It was total sex. Better. Better than sex."

Stephanie laughed out loud. "It doesn't last as long," she said.

Stephanie laughed so rarely that to hear a good old-fashioned girl laugh out of her was somehow reassuring. Maybe this was all normal after all. "I don't know about that," Darla said. "Jason's pretty good, but *some* of the guys I knew at school…"

Stephanie laughed again with delight. "Are you and Jason planning to have children?" she said. "I hope I'm not being rude." Stephanie blushed a little, another unusual sight. "It's partly why I asked you to come ski with me. I didn't want to ask in front of everybody else."

"Huh? I don't know. Jason and I haven't talked too much about the future. I know he likes kids though, so I wouldn't be surprised."

"A boy? Will you have a little boy? That's what I really would like to know."

Darla opened her mouth and closed it again. The weird edge had come back into Stephanie's voice.

"I'm going to have a little girl," Stephanie said, looking off into the distance. "You can have a little boy. Then they can be married. Right here in the Valley."

"Uh, maybe it's a little soon to be planning this stuff," Darla said. She suddenly remembered the scene of their burning car last night. She turned cold. "I mean, I'm not sure my dad is still interested in…"

"Let's do some trees," Stephanie said. "Remember: your skis are going to go where you look, so don't look *at* the trees. Look at the spaces between them. Pretend the trees aren't there."

With that Stephanie glided backward away from Darla, moving toward the trees with that effortless, magical motion. Darla wondered for a moment if Stephanie was going to ski through the trees backward. With Stephanie it seemed like anything could happen at anytime. At the last moment, however, she made a quick pirouette. There was a flash of white and silver and Stephanie disappeared into the dark green line.

Darla flattened her own skis onto the snow and let herself glide toward the forest. "Darla loves to ski!" she said aloud. She'd only skied trees once before, with Jason, and it had been a disaster: a broken collarbone and two weeks of not speaking to each other. Fortunately this slope was gentle and the snow was in perfect condition—soft enough so she could get a good edge on every turn, but not mushy.

The tree line approached, dense and dark. Don't look at the trees! Pretend they're not there! A funny thing for Stephanie to say. It seemed like they did a lot of pretending around here. Bucky Price seemed to be pretending that his Lodge was still full of the same happy skiers as it was five years ago and not a half-burnt haunted house. When they first met Stephanie, was pretending that her old boyfriend was still alive. She was still pretending, but did it count if he actually *was* alive? Had Stephanie known all along?

Don't look at the trees! Darla looked instead at the gap that Stephanie had disappeared into. She dipped her knees and made a few short turns on the open snow and then glided into the woods.

It's very hard to ski in a forest and not look at the trees but Darla kept focus, forcing herself to stare instead at the bright flashes of snow underfoot and glimpses of blue sky ahead. She kept to the same short rhythm she'd seen Stephanie use, turning and breathing quickly. A sharp branch snagged her wool cap but Darla kept going, skiing faster than she'd ever imagined she could through trees. Dark trunks nipped at her elbows and shoulders. You couldn't possibly pretend they weren't there as Stephanie had suggested. Darla instead thought of them as phantoms, ghosts, snakes under the bed that could only bother you if you let them.

A thicket approached and the slope steepened. Darla doubled her turns and it seemed like her heart rate doubled at the same time. Was she going the right way? She should be following Stephanie's tracks but was too busy not looking at trees to look at the ground.

Darla whooped and ducked. *That* was no phantom tree limb—it could have taken her head right off. Next time she was going to wear a helmet. Darla smiled. The trees were thinning, the gaps between them growing larger and she could see clear day light ahead. Next time: this run was so exhilarating that she wasn't even done with it and she couldn't wait to ski it again. Wait until she got Jason in here! Too bad the day was over. The shadows were long on the ground and the darkness growing deep in the trees.

"Darla!"

Darla flew out of the trees into the long afternoon light. She was on top of a small open bowl. Stephanie was a hundred feet below, waving her ski poles. Darla opened up her skis and let herself fall down the bowl, taking it in one steep Stephanie-like turn. Darla stopped at the bottom in a spray of snow and then collapsed.

"I'm dead," she said. "I'm totally dead."

"Are you okay? You were in there so long. I'm glad you took it easy, but it's getting late and we should make our way down to the village."

Darla sat up and unzipped her snow suit. She was drenched with sweat. "Take it easy?" she said. "Are you kidding? That's the fastest I've ever skied anything, I think."

"Fun, huh?"

"*So* fun. I did it just like you said and it worked! It totally worked. You're a great teacher, Stephanie. Whenever I try to get Jason to give me some tips…"

"Well, no offense but he's not a very good skier to begin with. He skis with his butt. But most guys don't ski very good. It's like they're trying to prove something to the mountain, beat it up or something. I used to tell Thad all the time that…"

Stephanie stopped and looked away quickly. They were near a granite outcropping that overlooked the Valley, already in shadow. Not far below was the dark bulk of the Lodge surrounded by Karnival tents.

"Stephanie?" Was she hiding tears? First laughter, then weird family planning, now tears. What *was* going on? She'd mentioned her brother Thad who'd been crippled in that same avalanche that Andy had been in. Darla's dad seemed to think that Andy had murdered Thad. Did Stephanie know something about this?

"Each man kills the think he loves," Stephanie said abruptly. Again, Darla had this weird feeling Stephanie was reading her mind. "That's by Oscar Wilde," Stephanie said. "Do you know Oscar Wilde?"

"Uh, no," Darla said. "I did more marketing stuff at Bennington. But what does it mean? Who was killed?"

"Why don't we take a break?" Stephanie said suddenly, clicking out of her skis. She sat down in the snow next to Darla but didn't look at her. Instead she continued to gaze steadily down the mountain toward the Lodge. Darla, though still hot from her exhilarating run, felt a chill on her back. The happy, natural Stephanie was gone completely. The other Stephanie was back. Darla stood up, kicked her own skis off and sat back down again.

"You know this is a very special place," Stephanie said. "You should know that."

Darla leaned forward to look. They were on the edge of what was basically a granite cliff, sprinkled with snow in only a few patches. The chill in her back turned over her whole body. "This isn't where, where…"

"No. Oh no. That happened on the other ridge. Little Spring Ridge over there on the other side of the valley." Stephanie pointed toward the far slope now in shadow. Dark birds circled over the far end.

"Oh."

"Do you know about Little Spring? Did Mr. Tescher tell you any of the history of Sunny Valley?

"Uh, a little. He said his great great grandfather…"

"This is where the Indian girl Little Spring and her husband waited for the Washoe men to come back from their hunting trip. Right here in the trees. She brought him here."

"Why?"

"It was the only way to kill the Washoe men. She knew it too. She knew about everything and everyone. When the men came back and found the women dead in the village they went crazy. They danced and shouted and cut themselves with their knives. Little Spring and Cor just sat here in this grove and watched. Isn't that romantic?"

"Uh,"

"Then when the Washoe were really worked up Little Spring told her husband what to do. He took his rifle and shot at them. The Washoe all looked up and saw Cor and Little Spring sitting here. The men were so mad they ran straight up the slope! Isn't that ridiculous? It was like they forgot they were Indians. Little Spring's husband just picked them off one by one. And then this was all hers, the whole valley. Isn't that a wonderful story? Mama used to tell it to me every year on Candle Night. That's what we used to call Karnival."

"So they just murdered…"

"I come up here all the time and think about Little Spring and her husband. How they protected each other. It's because of her that this is my valley now."

"Your valley? I thought…"

"Well, once I turn 21. Daddy runs everything right now. But I'm the sixth after Little Spring. Mama was the fifth. My little baby daughter will be next."

Darla bit her lip. Stephanie's daughter by whom? Andy the ghost? His voice came back to her, choked with bitterness. "She killed me. She'll pay for it." If Stephanie died before she had a daughter that would end the tradition. It would be the end of Little Spring's line. "Stephanie," Darla said, "I know you don't want to talk about Andy, but I really need to tell you…"

But Stephanie was up again, stepping into her bindings. "Are you ready? It's late and we really should get going." She looked up at the sky. "Gosh, it's almost dark already. We've got to get down to Karnival for the parade."

Darla stood and clicked in. There was no arguing with Stephanie when she was like this. She pushed her pole straps over her gloves and bent her knees a few times to warm them up.

"Ready?"

Darla turned. Stephanie was standing right at the granite ledge, her skis practically sticking out into empty space.

"Down there?" Darla said. "Stephanie, I can't ski that."

"Oh I know. It's my favorite run but you're not ready. We're going to follow the trees to the left here and join up with Nova, the big main run. Next year maybe. I just wanted to take a look."

"Next year! I wish. You're such a good teacher, though, Stephanie. I'd love to take some more lessons from you." Darla stopped. She was prattling away like this was another nice ski day. Their car had been burnt last night and they'd been imprisoned. Now night was falling and who knew what weird stuff was going to happen next. Instead of taking skiing lessons, Darla should be down in the village trying to figure out how to get away from this place.

"I'm ready, Stephanie," Darla said. She shivered. It was getting cold.

Stephanie planted her poles, but didn't move backward. In fact she leaned a little more forward over the cornice.

"Stephanie?"

Stephanie's mouth was open, her eyes wide. If ever Stephanie were to look afraid of something, Darla thought, this is how she'd look. What was she seeing down there? Darla inched forward but couldn't convince herself to get that close to the edge.

"What is it?" Darla chopped her poles into the snow, which was now beginning to crust over from the evening cold. "Shouldn't we…"

"Right down there," Stephanie said, in a voice Darla had not heard before. "Come here and take a look. Right down there at the bottom."

"What?" Darla inched forward. Stephanie grabbed her jacket and pulled her to the edge. "Look!" Stephanie said. "Can you see what's down there?"

Darla's heart was in her throat. She'd nearly lost balance when Stephanie grabbed her. She planted her poles and set her edges to keep herself from moving any further forward. She craned her neck as far as she could until she could see the bottom of the rocky chute below. The last rays of sun were trickling through the surrounding trees and glinting on something, something shiny and red. Something big, like a car. A car? How ever could any sort of car get down there? "What is it?" she said.

Stephanie planted her poles. "I've got to go down." Her voice was tiny, like a little girl's. "You go the other way, but I'll go down here. He might need help."

"Who might need help? Andy? Is he down there? What is that thing?"

"It's Daddy's Ski-Doo," Stephanie said, and launched herself into the dark space before them.

Chapter 37

Lance sprayed the last of the orange paint on to the snow. He was standing behind one of the massive snow banks that lined the edge of the parking lot, hard snow piled high by the plows over the winter. He shook the container, vigorously rattling the ball inside, and made one last test spray to make sure it was empty. "We use this shit to mark the race lanes," he said, and handed the can up to the girl who was sitting on his shoulders.

"You won, of course," April said. "What am I supposed to do with this?"

"Of course I won. Just breathe it. Spray it near your nose and breathe it in."

"Oh *right*. I'm going to get, like, orange paint all over my face."

"The paint is all gone. I sprayed it all out. Just breathe in what's left."

"You go first."

"I can't. I'll fall down and you'll get hurt. You first, then me."

Lance felt April sit up straight on his shoulders. There was a brief hiss of spray and a squeal. "Jeepers," she said. "This is what the total losers do back home."

"You want to get fucked up good for the parade," Lance said. "Just wait. It's worth it."

"Ooooo-weee! I think I'm going to fall off. Put me down."

Lance let April slide off his shoulders. As she came down she wrapped her legs around his waist and threw herself backwards. They both landed in the icy slush that covered the parking lot. "Oh you *brute*," April said.

"Take it easy." Lance stood up and brushed wet snow off his jeans.

"We're going to miss the parade."

April crawled up off the snow, weaving. She tucked herself under Lance's arm.

"How come you're not in the parade?" she said. "I thought you were, like, Mister Wile E. Coyote."

"I got a special excuse," he said. "It's 'cuz you're my date."

"So what happens anyway?"

"You'll see. I want it to be a surprise."

"I hate surprises," April said. "I think I'll go back and find the other kids."

"Hang on," Lance said, "You're a pushy bitch, aren't you?"

April slapped his shoulder. "You just figured that out. Congratulations."

Lance folded his arms across his chest. "It happens right here in the parking lot. The Coyotes build a bonfire and all the locals from up and down Highway 6 come here and throw shit in."

"How totally quaint."

"It used to be cooler. This girl Stephanie would go around the circle. All the women pulled their shirts up and she rubbed honey on their stomachs.

"Ooooh. What did she do to the guys?"

Lance stretched his neck. He looked at the packed snow bank behind them, now just a looming shadow. "She didn't do anything to the guys."

"Well, if *I* was the girl things would be a little different," April said. She reached for the spray paint can but Lance held it away.

"What?" she said.

"You gotta wait."

"I'm the pushy bitch, remember? I don't want to wait."

"I know that. But you gotta."

"Gimme just a little one."

Lance handed the can to April and heard her sniff and shake her head like a wet dog. From where they were, hidden behind the parking lot drifts, they could see the slopes of the ski area perfectly and hear the Karnival participants in the parking lot behind them. A little boy was crying for his mother and the group from the junior college were singing drunkenly:

Onward Christian soldiers, marching off to war

With the cross of Jesus going on before

Christ the royal Master, leads against the foe;

Forward into battle, see his banners go!

April giggled. "That's our school fight song," she said.

"You gotta lot of fights at your school?"

"No, stupid. It's like the football fight song. She threw a hand in the air and joined in the next verse:

At the sigh of triumph Satan's host doth flee;

On then, Christian soldiers, on to victory!

"Hey, hey shut up," Lance said. "People are going to hear us."

"I don't care if anyone hears us," April said and threw her head back to sing.

Hell's foundations quiver at the shout of praise;

Brothers, lift your voices, loud your anthems raise

"Shut up," Lance said. He pulled her close and put a rough hand to her mouth. "The parade's about to start anyway."

The valley was dark but they could see the outlines of the ski area and the wide main run down the center. An orange glow appeared at the very top of the mountain, like a rising moon. The glow grew and then seemed to splinter into fragments, individual orange stars.

"Now," Lance said. He held the aerosol can to April's face and sprayed. She closed her eyes and inhaled deeply. "Ooooh-weee," she said. Lance took three deep breaths and then inhaled from the spray can himself. "Mother fucker," he said.

The orange stars moved again, joining together on the ridge to make a new yellow sun. The sun twirled and then splintered. Three times it happened.

"Something's alive up there," April said. Lance coughed. He sprayed the can in April's face again. She laughed, but quietly. He felt her lean against him, as if her legs were getting weak. "It's alive, all right," Lance said. "It's alive and fucked up."

The orange stars separated again and began to fall down through the sky. Or were they drops of metal pouring out of something, drip after drip glowing with incredible heat? April was sure they were drips, molten drips, but then they began to curve in space. The drips curved gently to the left and then again to the right until the sky was filled with a bending, moving, orange blaze, an enormous flying snake burning with fire.

"What *is* it?" April said. Acid was rising in her throat and she was shaking. She grabbed at Lance, pushing her fingernails into his neck. "What *is* it?"

"Torches," Lance said. "Lotsa torches. Flying Coyotes skiing torch parade. Been doing it every year since people drove covered wagons." He took a whiff of the aerosol. "It's pretty, ain't it?"

"I hate it," April said. She buried her face in his neck. "It's going to burn us."

The snake had a tail now, a cluster of orange disappearing into black.

"Watch," Lance said, peeling April off his chest and holding her to face the mountain. "You better watch."

The line of fire turned and turned again, working its way down the mountain. April wondered if it would ignite the trees on the mountain and then the thick woods around the Lodge. "Is it coming here?" she said. "Is it coming for me?"

She put her gloved hands to her eyes.

"Yes ma'am," Lance said. "The Coyotes should all be here in about ten minutes. They all want to meet you." He pressed the spray can into April's hands. She took it unsteadily and then straightened.

"This is bad, bad stuff," she said.

"You know it."

Her fingers curled around the can, which was icy cold. She held it to the sky. "Here snakey snakey," she said. She brought it back to her face, sprayed, and inhaled deeply.

"Let's go baby," Lance said. He put his arms around April's shoulders to steer her toward the parking lot, toward the bonfire, but the weight was too much for her. She collapsed into the slush.

"Mother *fucker*," Lance said, and bent down to pick her up.

CHAPTER 38

I led the way up Little Spring Ridge. I could hear Thad's lungs rasping behind me. I could smell the vapor of Scotch and cigarettes in the steam rising off his shoulders. Thad had been on tour for nearly six months and hadn't done anything like this kind of climbing, but he seemed determined to keep up.

I stopped just below the granite step and took a drink of water from my flask. I didn't need it, but it gave Thad a chance to catch his breath. I offered him water but he refused.

"Why don't we just forget this, Andy," he said. "Let's go back and get some sleep."

I stowed my bottle and strapped on my ski poles. I had nothing to say. My destiny had been stolen from me. I had nowhere to go but up onto that ridge.

"C'mon. Or we can go down to the 'Butte for a few hours. Get some breakfast and then come back. Tell Bucky we had a great run."

"No."

Thad stood motionless in the snow. The sun was out now, shining hard on both of us, but Thad shivered. His lips quivered so much he could barely get the next words out. "He only wants one of us to come back. You know that?"

"I know it." A harsh silence fell, broken only by the sound of clumped snow dropping off the surrounding pine branches as the trees warmed. "Let's get it over with," Thad said finally. He pushed me aside and took the lead.

"I feel like I got bowling balls strapped on my feet instead of Telemark gear," he said over his shoulder. "It's like the oxygen's been sucked out of Sunny Valley."

We made the ridge and pulled off our skins. The sun was full on the new snow pack, melting the top crystals, heating the entire mass of snow all along the cornice. Thad glided down the flat top of the ridge and stopped a yard short of the edge. It was heating so fast I could hear the snow creaking under us, fissures widening in the tons of snow underfoot.

"Andy…"

"You afraid?" I stuck out my lower lip, mimicking the way Thad used to taunt me when I first learned to ski, when the greenest of Sunny Valley's green slopes looked to me like radical couloirs. He'd lured me out onto Sunny Valley's steepest runs many times, hoping, I was sure, that I would break my neck.

Thad laughed at my imitation and blew what air he had in his lungs out into the morning, creating a cloud of steam. "You stopped being afraid pretty fast," he said. "You ski the steeps better than anyone I ever saw who didn't grow up here."

"I had a good teacher."

"Stephanie? You're probably the only guy who ever actually listened to her. Most guys just watch her ass."

"I did that too."

The line of trees behind Thad suddenly dumped snow, filling the morning stillness with a series of thuds. Thad crept forward on his skis but then stopped. "You know I don't care about you and Steph," he said. "That's all Bucky's bullshit. I don't care if you guys get married."

"I know."

He turned. His face was full of pain. "Then why are we doing this? Why are we going to make this fucking drop? The whole face is going to cut loose any minute now. You and I got nothing to prove. Nothing to work out. We're both up here acting like cowboys because of what happened a hundred years ago. Let's just shake hands and ski back through the trees. If Bucky gives us any shit we'll kick his ass. You and me. We could do it."

I bent down and tightened the buckles of my boots.

"Really, Ass..I mean Andy," Thad said. "We don't need to do this. You don't need to do it. You got your whole life…"

"I've got nothing," I said. "Stephanie and I were meant to be together. Forever. To protect each other. But she sold me so she could go to the Olympics. If I'm nothing to her, than I am nothing. My life is over. I can't go back to the Valley."

I planted a pole and took a high jump off the cornice. For a moment I was in the air, entirely free. What if death was like this? Air, adrenaline, freedom. No promises, no loneliness, no hunger. I made broad turns across the face, the most dangerous kind of turn to make in these conditions because they could literally saw the slab loose from the mountain. At the bottom of the couloir I planted and made a high jump turn, both skis arcing in the air nearly over my head. It was a move right out of Thad's last ski video. I knew he was watching.

There was a flat spot at the bottom of the couloir. I stopped there and looked back up the near vertical chute. Stephanie had taught me how to feel the forces of the mountain and I could feel them now. The entire slab above me was moving, pulsing imperceptibly downward. The snow mass thumped, like a heart, like living, breathing, death.

Thad, standing at the top of the chute, had no choice. He planted, turned, and launched himself over the edge.

CHAPTER 39

"Good night folks! Thanks for coming! Hope you had a good Karnival!" Carlie, the night cashier, waved a mittened hand as the last station wagon left the lodge parking lot and turned on to Highway 6. She cupped her hands around her mouth and shouted again. "Drive careful," she said. "It's slippy out there."

The day had been sunny but that meant scary driving after the shadows grew long and the wet patches of melted snow froze into little skating rinks on the sharp corners of Highway 6. Carlie sighed and put her hands on her hips, watching the line of cars head down the highway, their red taillights glowing like demon eyes. They were flatlanders, sure, but most had been regular visitors to Sunny Valley in the years before the drought. They would know about the road.

Carlie turned and walked back toward the Lodge. The torchlight parade was over and Tescher's boys were tearing the pavilions apart, piling the wood into the center of the parking lot for the bonfire. Carlie lit a cigarette and inhaled deeply. They'd started up Candle Night again a few years ago, but she didn't look forward to it anymore, not like she did when she was little. Back then, standing in the circle with all the other women from the neighboring mountain towns had made her feel special, part of a special club. Now with Caroline gone and all the nastiness of the last four years it was just angry and dark. Some folk still came but they sure didn't bring their kids. Carlie just wanted to get it over with and get back down the hill to Pine Butte.

Two shapes came forward out of the gloom: the sheriff in his bulky grey jacket and one of the Chilean boys, the handsome one named Alejandro. He had his coyote mask pushed up on top of his head. Both the sheriff and the boy were carrying orange highway cones.

"You need to get going yourself, Carlie," said the sheriff. "Head back down before it gets too cold."

"But they're burning tonight," Carlie said. "Aren't they burning tonight?"

The sheriff handed his stack of cones to Alejandro. "Go ahead, son," he said. "Get started. Leave a lane for a few folks to get out."

The dark-eyed boy took the cones and kept walking, weaving slightly.

The sheriff turned back to Carlie, put his hands in his pockets and looked at his shoes. "Lance told me it's only locals tonight, Carl," he said.

"I'm local," Carlie said. "I'm local as anybody. My folks been coming since before the Lodge was built. They even been inside the old cabin."

A sharp wind whipped off the ski mountain and blew across the parking lot. Carlie and the sheriff both turned their backs to it, hitching their collars up against the cold.

"Gettin' icy," the sheriff said. He straightened back up and adjusted his hat. "I know you're local, Carlie. Lance and the boys don't want *nobody* up here tonight. I gotta go too. You imagine that? Soon as I get those church folks out of here, I'm going down too."

Carlie lifted her chin, beckoning the sheriff closer. He leaned down. "Is it because of *him*?" Carlie whispered. "'Cuz he's back and all? Are they going to do something to him?"

The sheriff took off his hat, turned it around twice in his hands and put it back on. Carlie remembered how as a little boy his folks called him "The Whipper" for the way he liked to grab the big grey squirrels by the tail and whip their heads against a stump. She'd never seen him look the way he did now, his forehead creased so deep. And she'd never seen him take his hat off in public.

"I don't know, Carlie," he said. "I tried to find out but nobody's talking. I ain't seen Tescher all day and Price holed up somewheres after the races were over. I can't even find Stephanie."

"Sheriff! Sheriff!" It was the church group leader. Another icy wind shot across the parking lot, carrying his voice away.

"What're you going to do about them?" Carlie said. The sheriff shrugged. "Bus tires are all slashed. Tescher's boys want those kids up here tonight but I don't know. That's going too far."

"Sheriff!" The group leader called again. "Have you heard anything yet?"

"Son?"

"About the tow truck. To get us back down the mountain. I've got most of my young people assembled and ready."

"Son, if the tow truck ain't here yet they ain't coming."

The church leader pressed his lips together and looked back over his shoulder. The wood pile being assembled by a dozen men in coyote masks was now as high as the disabled school bus. "We could stay at the Lodge, I suppose. The cost is prohibitive."

"The Lodge is closed," Carlie said. "We're always closed for Karnival."

"Really? I imagine it would be your busiest night. Sheriff, what *can* we do?"

The sheriff looked at Carlie, who looked back. "How many kids you got?" he said.

"Twelve. They're all on the bus except one young lady whom I believe…"

"Can you take a few Carlie? I can squeeze seven or eight into the Blazer. You take the rest?"

"Oh sure. I take more than that when we go to the Tracy drive-in."

"Okay then, preacher. That's what we're doing."

"I'm not a preacher, sheriff. I'm only the recreation coordinator."

"It doesn't matter. Carlie and I will pull up to the bus. The kids will get in and we'll go. And we're doing this right now, understand?"

"Certainly, Sheriff. As I said, there's one young lady who…"

Alejandro staggered up out of the dark. He was carrying no highway cones and his coyote mask was pulled down on his face. He walked past them without recognition.

"You got five minutes," the sheriff said. "Get your kids in the cars. Don't you worry about your young lady." The Sheriff looked back toward the growing pyre and the crowd around it. He adjusted his hat. "I'll make sure she's taken care of," he said.

CHAPTER 40

"Darla!"

Two figures called from the far side of the parking lot. Darla kicked off her skis and walked toward them, her stiff ski boots feeling awkward on the slushy asphalt. The exhilaration of her runs with Stephanie were long gone, replaced by a sense of dread as night fell on the Valley. "Dad?" Darla called out as she crossed the parking lot. "Jason?"

Jason took her gloved hands. "It's so late, Squeaker. I was getting worried. Where have you been? What happened?"

"I'm not sure exactly. Stephanie took a different route down the mountain. I waited for her on the main run for a while but she never showed up." Darla looked around. "I guess Karnival's over," she said. On the far side of the parking lot masked men were using axes to break up the wooden pavilions. She put her hand to her mouth. "Oh shit."

"That's right," Jason said.

"Darla, Jason," Wallace Collins said, his voice quavering. "I've made a terrible mistake. Price and Tescher have worked together to defraud me. We must get away from this place as soon as possible. Darla, I don't know how I could have let you go off on your own."

"But everything seemed so *normal* this morning," Darla said. "Did you talk to Mr. Price or Mr. Tescher? Did you get your check back?"

Collins wrapped his arms around his sides. "Price gave me the brush off when we found him. He said he was busy with the ski races because Tescher was off somewhere drunk. He promised to help me deal with Tescher and then find us a ride down the mountain."

"Well, that's good," Darla said.

"But we haven't seen him since," Jason said. "We watched the races and then came down here for the torchlight parade. Now all the cars are gone and he's still not here."

A picture formed in Darla's mind, the bright red snowmobile smashed in the rocks and Stephanie skiing down the steep slope toward it. Darla had watched her search around the broken snowmobile for only a few minutes before taking off again, flying down the mountain as if chased by demons.

"I don't think we can't count on Mr. Price," Darla said. "Let me look around the parking lot. I'll see if there is anyone who can take us down. Or maybe I can find Stephanie."

"No, Darla. I forbid it. We must all stay together. We must find Kyle."

Voices rose on the far side of the parking lot. The Flying Coyotes torchlight parade had arrived. Laughing and cheering, the masked skiers formed a circle around the wood pit and held their torches high. Wallace Collins put his head in his hands. "Pride. Pride," he said. "This is all retribution for my sins of pride."

"Looks like someone got hurt," Jason said.

The last Coyote didn't stop to kick his skis off at the edge of the asphalt as the others had done. He skated forward across the parking lot with his skis grating loudly on the hard surface. He held no ski poles but pulled instead on the handles of a red emergency tow sled, one of the sleds used by ski patrollers to bring injured skiers down the mountain. A gray man-sized bundle was in the sled, held down by protective webbing.

The skier pushed his way to the torch-lit circle. Cheers and howls rose up and torches waved. The flames showed that the skier wore a grey coyote mask like everyone else but Darla recognized the worn blue jacket. It was Andy. As she watched he dropped the handles of the sled and threw his hands in the air, not so much in victory but as if reaching for some impossibly high point in the sky.

"Please," said Wallace Collins. "We should at least get out of sight." Limping painfully, he pulled Darla and Jason behind one of the tall snow banks at the edge of the parking lot and then slumped down to the ground. He leaned against the snow mound and closed his eyes. "Pray to God they don't find us."

"But what is Andy *doing*?" Darla said. "Who is in the rescue sled? What if it's Stephanie? He said he was going to kill her. I can't let that happen."

"Squeaker," said Jason," we just gotta get away from these people. We've got to save our own necks."

Darla kicked at the snow mound with her ski boots and made a step for herself so she could climb up and look over the top. Cheers and howls rose up around the bonfire. A half dozen Coyotes took axes to the Lodge itself, hacking away the shingled exterior and exposing the log structure underneath. A chainsaw growled to life and two carved logs that supported the shingled entryway collapsed.

Andy, still standing near the wood pyre, dropped his arms and looked over with alarm. "Hey," he said, "stay away from there. Stay away from the Lodge."

The Coyotes gathered around Andy. Their torches lit the parking lot and the Lodge with a flickering glow. Andy's face looked deeply lined, savage in the torchlight.

Jason joined Darla on top of the snow bank. "We should get out of here before this gets any weirder," he said.

"Where are we going to go?" Darla said.

Wallace Collins stirred. "Kyle is still out there. My son. You've got to find him."

Darla turned. "Forget it, Dad," she said. "It's too dangerous for any of us to go wandering around right now. I don't know what happened to Kyle but he's a big boy. He's been up here all winter and he knows his way around better than we do. I'm not going to risk my life—or yours, Dad—to go chase that loser through the snow."

Collins leaned back, his jaw set and lips pursed. "I've lost a fortune," he said. "Kyle is all I have left."

"We could walk up to Tescher's," Jason said, looking doubtfully up the snowy trail behind them that led into the dark woods. "He would help us."

"I'm not going out there," Darla said. "And I don't trust that guy either. At least here we're in the light and we can see what's going on."

Wallace Collins stirred and opened his eyes. "Darla's right," he said.

"Tescher's as bad as anyone here. I should know." He leaned back against the dirty snow and waved a hand, gesturing toward the bonfire. "This is all my fault. I've brought this upon us. If we're going to feel the flames of hell, it's my fault."

"Dad, this isn't really helping."

"I made a pact with the Devil. With two Devils. I thought I was doing good. I wanted to help these people. Now I see I was tricked by Satan."

"Dad, be *quiet*. I need to figure out what's happening."

"I knew that boy, Andy. He worked our lifts at Presserton. I spoke with him several times. It was he who told me about Sunny Valley, about the drought. He knew Tescher was broke and needed to sell the mountain. It was his idea to try to break Price, to force Price to sell the Lodge."

"You knew Andy?" Darla said. "Back home?"

Collins sighed. "The boy had lovely words about the place, a poem he'd written:

> *The night of storms has gone*
> *The sunshine bright and clear*
> *Gives glory to our Valley's dawn*
> *And sparks the winter air"*

A roar rose up. Coyote voices yelled and howled. Darla and Jason climbed higher on the snow bank to watch.

The large logs sawed from the outside of the Lodge had been added to the pyre. The fire was lit but still burning only at the edges. Andy unwrapped the bundle from the emergency sled and was now carrying it to the top of the pyre.

Darla gasped. "It's Mr. Price."

"Is he dead?" Jason said.

"He's not moving."

Coyote howls filled the night air and torches were thrown at Andy's feet. Now Lance was on the pyre too, holding a girl limp in his arms. He set her down on the stack of wood next to the inert body of Bucky Price.

"And Stephanie," Jason said.

"No," Darla said. "That's not her. I don't know who that is."

"Death to the old," Lance yelled at the crowd, his voice loud, manic. "And death to the new. This is our Valley now. It's THE END."

Coyotes chanted: "Our VALLEY. Our VALLEY. Our VALLEY."

A blast of wind swept the lot, carrying snow and sand and fanning the flames higher. It also carried Andy's voice. Though he was on the far side of the parking lot, on top of the wooden pyre, Darla and Jason could hear him as clearly as if he was whispering into their ears.

> *Death, death is my joy*
> *I long to be at rest*
> *I wish the cold earth*
> *To hold this desolate breast.*

"He's out of his tree," Jason said. "He's going to burn himself too."

Darla jumped up and scrambled over the snow bank. "He *can't*," she said. "he *can't* do that. He can't *burn*."

The Coyotes howled in unison, linking their wailing calls into a single undulating siren. The flames grew, illuminating the faces of both Andy and Lance.

Darla ran across the parking lot. She reached the edge of the ring of Coyotes. She tried to push her way through but she was grabbed from behind and thrown forward. She landed sprawling at the base of the wood pile. Another coyote-masked figure took a 2x4 from the pyre. It burned on one end. Darla saw the burning club rise up, saw the cruel dispassion of the flame-lit coyote mask above her. Wind blew, and blew again, and for a moment all Darla could see was flame.

CHAPTER 41

Is hell so cold, so very cold? I open my eyes but see only black. I can move neither legs nor arms but that is no surprise: I've been frozen my whole life, locked in a state between being and not being, breathing and not breathing.

I try to inhale. Something is in my mouth, stuffing it so hard that my jaws ache. Something forcing its way inside me, stealing my breath and soul. I cough, convulse, work my jaws in desperation. My mouth is full of rocks and sand. I twist and try to spit, try to free my tongue. Finally the mass loosens, recedes, dissolves. I spit successfully. It is not rocks and sand. My mouth is filled with snow.

As are my ears, eyelids and nostrils. There is snow between my legs, snow up my ass. There was an avalanche and I was in it. I'm still in it. I try to move my arms, to push away the weight of snow but they are locked.

Hell then, is snow. I've known it since I came to Sunny Valley. Beautiful in the sky, in photos, sprinkled in the trees. Deadly when it is on the ground. Deadly when a flatlander loses a ski on the back side of the mountain on the last run of the day. The sun sets and the lifts stop running. The flatlander is left thrashing desperately through the woods in snow so deep that it takes nearly an hour to move a hundred yards. It's not long before he's so exhausted he can only lay his sweat-soaked body onto the snow to die.

Deadliest, like so many things, when it's at its most beautiful. After a big storm covers the mountain in fresh drifts and the sun comes out to light the world of white and blue. When skiers tumble out of the lodges like children on Christmas day, proud of their fat skis and orange trailing ribbons, anxious to ski the deadly snow. Deadly because the hot daggers of the sun stab the ridges, finding stress points in the massive snow packs and weakening them. Snow flakes are desperate lovers—they cling to each other with surprising strength. You can build bridges of snow—houses, airplane runways. But a tiny needle of sunlight destroys that bond in an instant and a whole mountain collapses under its own weight.

Snow is terrible, but it is weak. As I am weak. Will I be the weakest person in hell, the most pathetic, the man who begged for love on any terms only to be murdered by it?

Noise. A thump deep in my chest like a heartbeat. It grows louder and more forceful. Is my heart finally rebelling, trying to break its way out of the cage? Louder, deeper, it shakes me, shakes my snowy prison. Now a deafening heartbeat, now an angry whining growl in my ears.

The growl: a snowmobile. The thud: a helicopter. I'm not dead.

My arms won't move. I try to kick, push with my knees against the snow but only my right leg has any strength. Still, the snow yields a little. I kick again, kick, punch with my shoulders and head. The snow around me, rock hard but softened by the morning sun, begins to splinter. I kick and thrash and now my right arm is up in front of me, clawing at the snow. There are blue lines, then white, then sun. With a final heave I sit up into blinding sunshine. I was buried by only a foot or two of snow.

The thump, the whine. I look up-slope and see a helicopter clearing the trees, heading down the mountain, probably for Pine Butte. In the middle of the clearing a man on a red Ski-Doo guns the engine and watches the helicopter disappear. When it's gone he stays, looking carefully over the chaotic ice blocks of the collapsed hillside. He's only a few yards away and I can see him clearly. It's my father. It's Bucky Price.

It's all I can do to lift my one working arm and make a feeble wave. Bucky is looking the other way but finally his eyes, still searching, find me. For a moment we look at each other with complete comprehension and I understand something that had puzzled me the night before. Bucky could have killed me outright any time in the last nine years, any time after Caroline, his wife, died. He could have faked an accident or claimed I ran away. Anyone would have believed him, even Stephanie. Why risk Thad's life?

Thad had said last night that Bucky was afraid to openly break his promise to Caroline. As if she could still reach him from her grave up on Little Spring Ridge. As if her sad, weak bones gnawed away by cancer could still find vengeance, find justice. He couldn't kill me outright.

At first he tried to drive me away with cruelty, but it was too late—Stephanie had taken hold of my heart. This avalanche was an accident, perhaps a loophole that Bucky hoped would release him from his compact with the dead.

Now, lying paralyzed in the murderous snow, I realize he had at least given me a chance. This was a test, a challenge for the heir of Sunny Valley. A test that perhaps Thad and I have both failed.

Price guns the snowmobile and starts it into motion. He turns two tight circles and then heads off toward the tree line, away from me. He's not going to get help. The thudding helicopter won't return. I don't care.

I fight my way up out of the snow. My left arm is completely dead and my left leg nearly so. It's three miles to Highway 6 and my skis are lost. I take one step and collapse. I struggle upwards again, take another step and fall again. I am full of pain, but I will cross the avalanche field. I will make it to Highway 6. I'm leaving, but I'll come back to this icy hell. I know the story now. I know how to take the Valley for my own. All that's needed are fire and death. With one arm completely paralyzed and one leg nearly so, I'm half a man, or less, but all of me will come back.

CHAPTER 42

"*Stop* that." A voice came from behind. The Coyote who stood over Darla turned his head and then lowered the flaming board in his hands..

"Stop. *Everyone* stop." The crowd opened and Darla saw a white and silver flash. It was Stephanie, who pushed her way through the crowd impatiently.

She ignored Darla and looked up onto the woodpile. "What are you doing?" she said. "It's not time to burn yet. We haven't done the ceremony or anything."

Darla scrambled to her feet. "Stephanie, they want to kill you! They're starting their own ceremony!"

"Get *down* from there," Stephanie said. "And bring Daddy and that girl."

Silence fell over the parking lot. Only a breath of wind and the restless popping of the burning edge of the fire could be heard.

"It's OVER," someone finally yelled from the back of the crowd. "This is our Valley now."

"It's not over." Stephanie turned to face the Coyotes, her jacket lit red by the rising fire. "It never will be over. Andy came back for *me*. Because he loves me. We're going to get married and have a baby. A little girl. It never will be over."

Andy stood at the top of the pyre. He was still as an ice sculpture. His eyes were closed and arms folded.

"Come down Andy," Stephanie said.

"BURN HER TOO." The voice, which came from the back of the Coyotes, was quickly caught in the wind and blown away.

Stephanie turned again. "Are you stupid? Don't you remember what happened when Daddy and Mr. Tescher tried to trick me? When they tried to take the Valley away from me? To take Andy away from me? Don't you want snow? Don't you want winter? Or do you just want mud? Because that's all you're going to have without me. Mud."

The ring of Coyotes fell silent. Stephanie started to sing.

"Aah-aah. Aaah- Aaah."

The girl at the top of the pyre sat up and put her face in her hands. "Get her down please," Stephanie said. Her eyes were closed tight as she sang. "She's not going to do you any good."

Coyotes stepped forward and pushed some of the burning wood away, helping April step unsteadily onto the parking lot.

"Aah-aaha. Aaah-aaah. Now Andy you get down too. And bring Daddy with you. We'll get married right now. Tonight. We'll stand on the holy fireplace in the Lodge. Right where Grandma and Grandpa are buried. They will marry us. Don't you see?"

Andy was still motionless atop the pyre, his face half-lit by the flames that crept near his feet. Stephanie faced again the circled Coyotes. Only her eyes were lit. "Where's your leader?" she said. "Where's Mr. Tescher? Why isn't *he* here?"

The Coyotes remained silent.

"He's not here because he's dead." She pointed up, over the Lodge. "His body is up on Little Spring Ridge. Right where my mama is buried. Andy killed him. He did it for me. He *protected* me, just like he's supposed to."

"Kill her!" A torch flew out of the crowd. It landed near Stephanie's feet but then skittered away on the wet asphalt.

"I know Andy killed Daddy too," Stephanie said. She took two difficult breaths. "That's because I told him to. He promised me he would and now that promise is done. He did it for me. Not for you."

Wind stirred the flames and they crackled higher. "Come down Andy," Stephanie said. Andy still stood in the flames, his face streaming with tears. "Come down now."

Slowly, with painful steps, Andy climbed off the pyre.

A sudden gust of icy wind pushed the flames up behind him. The body of Bucky Price was engulfed.

CHAPTER 43

I broke into a summer cabin and with my one good hand built a fire in the wood stove. I lay near it and felt the heat enter and restore me. I did not sleep, nor was I awake. I lived on the heat, on the flames.

On the second day the fingers on my left hand began to tingle. The tingles became pin pricks and then needles and then hot lava. Pain seared my left arm and then extended down to my chest, groin, and leg. I screamed that night, filled the flimsy cabin with the loudest sound ever made by a human voice. I screamed until my throat bled. It was only partly because of the pain in my limbs. It was also the pain of years, of my entire life. Finally the black seeds planted deep inside my soul could emerge.

I stayed in the cabin for four days, living on heat. The shooting pains stopped. I could again move my left hand and left leg, though with difficulty. There was no mirror, no shiny surface where I could look at myself, but I needed no mirror to know that my face was affected too: frozen, still caught under the murderous avalanche.

I thought of Stephanie. In a poem, Oscar Wilde says every man kills the thing he loves. She brought me to life and then killed me. Did that mean, then, that she loved me? I loved her, I would never question it. Did that mean, then, that I would kill her as well? Would I use the knife that I bought and honed for her father on her own perfect flesh?

After four days I limped to the highway and caught a ride with skiers heading down the mountain. They took me south to one of the big cities on the flatland. One offered me a couch to sleep on if I would watch his back while he sold drugs. I killed a man, an enormous biker, and went to Texas to hide. I worked in an open-pit copper mine on a blasting crew, reducing a holy mountain to dust.

I killed the foreman, and fled again. To a small town in Vermont. Back to the murderous snow.

CHAPTER 44

Strong hands reached down and pulled Darla to her feet. It was Jason.

"Let's get out here," he said. His eyes searched the glow around them. Two dozen Coyotes, in their masks, stood nearby, some with burning torches, though many had gone out. They were silent now. The howling and the shouting were gone.

"We can't," Darla said.

"Forget about that Andy guy. He's just another maniac like everyone else here."

"That's not it." Darla said again. She pulled Jason close and put her lips to his ear. "Look over there. Behind Andy. Look at the guy right behind him."

Jason looked at the cluster of masked figures behind Andy. All wore red ski patrol jackets except one jacket was more orange than red. The Coyote with the orange jacket stood with a very familiar slouch.

"That's Kyle!"

"Shhhh. I know."

"What is he…"

"Shhhhh. We might get him in trouble or something."

"That idiot."

A light snow began to fall, causing the remaining torches to splutter. Stephanie held her arms up to the sky and sang: "Ah-la. Ah-la. See?" she said, "Everything is fine now. Better than before. You don't need a new girl." Stephanie pointed at April, standing unsteadily near the bonfire. "Andy and I will get married. Won't we Andy?"

Andy had said nothing since Stephanie had pushed her way into the circle but now with sudden violence he ripped off his blue jacket and shirt, standing nearly white against the dimming firelight. A knife gleamed in his hands.

"I loved you," he said. The right side of his face was creased deeply with shadow. "I had nothing else, no one else, in this world. I can *have* nothing else." He opened his arms wide and walked toward Stephanie. The knife was ready.

Stephanie turned her back to him and faced the Lodge, singing again and waving her hands in the air. Snow was falling steadily now. The embers of the bonfire hissed in complaint. "C'mon," she said over her shoulder. "We'll be married. All we need to do is stand on the right spot."

Stephanie continued walking toward the Lodge, still singing, her voice gentle in the darkening night. Andy took one step towards her, then another. The knife dropped from his hands. "No, Stephanie," he said. He struggled forward, as if trying to move against a powerful wind. "NO…"

Kyle stepped out of the ring of Coyotes and scooped up the knife. He sprang onto Andy's back and slashed wildly. The blade ran across Andy's forehead and face, leaving a dark line of blood. Andy shook Kyle off and ran toward the Lodge. He tried to call for Stephanie but his mouth was filled with blood. Stephanie did not look back but walked calmly through the wrecked atrium and opened the front door.

Andy was only a few steps behind Stephanie when Kyle attacked again, jabbing the knife into Andy's shoulder as Andy struggled to enter the Lodge. The two of them disappeared through the log door and into the inky blackness inside.

"Kyle!" Wallace Collins scrambled forward, limping painfully toward the Lodge. He had nearly reached the door when he tripped over the scattered wreckage of the shingle awning.

Darla and Jason started to follow but then stopped. The Lodge, it seemed, had become a living thing. The windows now glowed yellow, like the eyes of a contented cat. The black doorway had turned shining white and welcoming. Darla inhaled, completely disoriented. What was this new vision, this new light? Then she lost her breath entirely as the windows, doors, logs and shingles of the Lodge heaved up and out in a massive explosion of flame and heat.

Darla flew backwards, knocking Jason over. Her hair and eyebrows singed and a tremendous heat washed over her face, an incredible, tearing pain. Her skin seemed to be at the point of blistering, but then the heat lifted.

The entire Lodge was in flames. The explosion collapsed the lower floors but the upper Lodge and roof still stood, floating over the fire. The heat, while not as bad as the initial blast, was still intense and growing. Most of the Flying Coyotes had been knocked to the ground but Darla could see they were now getting to their feet and running away into the fire-lit woods as if pursued by demons.

Darla stood up. She carefully touched her lips, her forehead, pushing away ashes and tears.

Jason still lay on the ground but he was conscious. Darla rushed to his side. Jason pointed a hand toward the fire. "Look," he said. "LOOK."

Darla looked back toward the burning Lodage. Two figures, a man and a woman, stood at a top-floor window, silhouetted by flames. As Darla watched they faced each other, holding hands as if in sacred marriage. Darla blinked, shook her head, and the vision was gone, consumed by the raging fire.

"LOOK," Jason said. He was trying to get up, trying to scramble toward the Lodge.

Darla, her face still aching from the heat, squinted at what had been the front door and saw her father crawling toward them. His clothes had been mostly blown off. He was little more than a black and red stain moving painfully over the parking lot.

Darla ran forward, grabbed Collins under his arms and pulled, dragging him away from the fire. Jason came forward to help. Collins screamed with pain but by the time they had him pulled to safety he had fallen silent.

"Dad! Dad!"

Jason dropped down to his knees. "Jesus, Darla, he's really burned. Look at his face."

"Oh...god. His *eyes* are bleeding. Is he even alive? Dad, can you hear me?"

Collins's lips, the skin charred and peeling, moved slightly. "Kyle..." he said. Jason bent down to hear Collins's words and then sat up again.

"What did he say?"

"Nothing. He's asking about your brother."

Darla bit her lip. "Kyle's okay, Dad. Don't worry about him." She unzipped her jacket. "Let's wrap him up or he's going to freeze to death."

"And then what?"

"We'll put him in that thing." She pointed to the red emergency sled that had held the body of Bucky Price. "And tow him up to Tescher's." She squinted into the snow banks around the edge of the parking lot, fiercely lit by the burning Lodge. "There's got to be a working Ski-doo around here somewhere."

"It's terrible, Darla. His face, his eyes…"

Wallace Collins groaned. "I can't see anything," he said.

Darla stood up and brushed the wet slush and ash from her ski pants. "You never will, Dad," she said.

ACKNOWLEDGEMENTS

Special thanks to: The Drunken Goats, Miki Terasawa, David Booth, Ann Jastrab, Maya Kovskaya, Andrew O. Dugas, Priti Vora, Todd Zuniga, and Opium Magazine.

ABOUT THE AUTHOR

Writer and photographer Vince Donovan lives in San Francisco. He winters in a small ski town in the high Sierra which he prefers not to name. His other novels include *Garage Love*, inspired by the life of Kurt Cobain, and *The Californiad*, an epic tale of the Golden State.